"Luke, if I go with you, they'll get the wrong idea about us."

"And what idea is that?"

"They'll think we're a couple," Jillian replied. "I know this seems odd, but I didn't come here to find a husband."

He appeared to be holding on to his frustration by a thread. "Let me get this straight. You saw the ad for Bachelor Gulch, so you moved here. But you aren't looking for a husband."

Glancing at all of the townsfolk who were watching their little interaction, Jillian considered walking away without saying another word. But how would it look to have the new girl in town stomp on his huge ego in front of more than a dozen residents?

In a voice meant for his ears alone, she said, "I'm really not in the market, Luke. But believe me, if I were, you'd be my first choice." And with quiet assurance, she stood on tiptoe to whisper a kiss against his cheek, then turned and left him in the middle of the street, staring after her.

Dear Reader,

The month of June makes me think of June brides, Father's Day and the first bloom of summer love. And Silhouette Romance is celebrating the start of summer with six wonderful books about love and romance.

Our BUNDLE OF JOY this month is delivered by Stella Bagwell's *The Tycoon's Tots*—her thirtieth Silhouette book. As her TWINS ON THE DOORSTEP miniseries continues, we finally discover who gets to keep those adorable babies...*and* find romance in the bargain.

Elizabeth August is back with her much-loved SMYTHESHIRE, MASSACHUSETTS series. In *The Determined Virgin* you'll meet a woman whose marriage of convenience is proving to be very *in*convenient, thanks to her intense attraction to her "in-name-only" husband.

BACHELOR GULCH is a little town that needs women, *and* the name of Sandra Steffen's brand-new miniseries. The fun begins in *Luke's Would-Be Bride* as a local bachelor falls for his feisty receptionist—the one woman in town *not* looking for a husband!

And there are plenty more compelling romances for you this month: A lovely lady rancher can't wait to hightail it out of Texas—till she meets her handsome new foreman in Leanna Wilson's *Lone Star Rancher*. A new husband can't bear to tell his amnesiac bride that the baby she's carrying isn't his, in *Her Forgotten Husband* by Anne Ha. And one lucky cowboy discovers a night of passion has just made him a daddy in Teresa Southwick's *The Bachelor's Baby*.

I hope you enjoy all of June's books!

Melissa Senate,
Senior Editor

Silhouette Romance

Please address questions and book requests to:
Silhouette Reader Service
U.S.: 3010 Walden Ave., P.O. Box 1325, Buffalo, NY 14269
Canadian: P.O. Box 609, Fort Erie, Ont. L2A 5X3

LUKE'S WOULD-BE BRIDE

Sandra Steffen

Silhouette
ROMANCE™
Published by Silhouette Books
America's Publisher of Contemporary Romance

For my brother, Ron Rademacher—
Sometimes the greatest heroes are the quietest ones.
I thought you'd always be here, buddy.
Save me a place in heaven, okay?

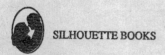 SILHOUETTE BOOKS

ISBN 0-373-19230-4

LUKE'S WOULD-BE BRIDE

Copyright © 1997 by Sandra E. Steffen

This edition published by arrangement with Harlequin Books S.A.

Printed in U.S.A.

Books by Sandra Steffen

Silhouette Romance

Child of Her Dreams #1005
*Bachelor Daddy #1028
*Bachelor at the Wedding #1045
*Expectant Bachelor #1056
Lullaby and Goodnight #1074
A Father for Always #1138
For Better, For Baby #1163
†Luke's Would-Be Bride #1230

*Wedding Wager
†Bachelor Gulch

Silhouette Desire

Gift Wrapped Dad #972

Silhouette Special Edition

Not Before Marriage! #1061

SANDRA STEFFEN

Creating memorable characters is one of Sandra's favorite aspects of writing. She's always been a romantic, and is thrilled to be able to spend her days doing what she loves—bringing her characters to life on her computer screen.

Sandra grew up in Michigan, the fourth of ten children, all of whom have taken the old adage "Go forth and multiply" quite literally. Add to this her husband, who is her real-life hero, their four school-age sons who keep their lives in constant motion, their gigantic cat, Percy, and her wonderful friends, in-laws and neighbors, and what to do you get? Chaos, of course, but also a wonderful sense of belonging she wouldn't trade for the world.

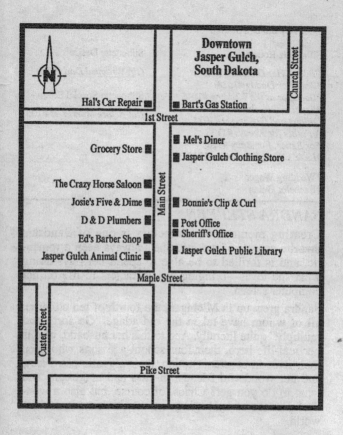

Downtown Jasper Gulch, South Dakota

N

Church Street

Hal's Car Repair ▪ ▪ Bart's Gas Station

1st Street

Grocery Store ▪
Main Street
The Crazy Horse Saloon ▪
Josie's Five & Dime ▪
D & D Plumbers ▪
Ed's Barber Shop ▪
Jasper Gulch Animal Clinic ▪

▪ Mel's Diner
▪ Jasper Gulch Clothing Store

▪ Bonnie's Clip & Curl
▪ Post Office
▪ Sheriff's Office
▪ Jasper Gulch Public Library

Maple Street

Custer Street

Pike Street

Chapter One

Luke Carson reached for his black bag with one hand and his black Stetson with the other, then hurried toward the door. The telephone started to ring before he'd taken his second step. Shoving his hat on his head and his bag under one arm, he grabbed the receiver and bit back a curse.

"Jasper Gulch Animal Clinic."

He was vaguely aware of the bead of perspiration trailing down the side of his neck, but most of his attention was trained on Butch Brunner's voice on the other end of the line. "You gotta get here as soon as possible, Luke. This is the second steer to take sick this week."

While Butch talked on, Luke glanced at his watch and rummaged through the clutter on his desk. He never thought he'd see the day when he actually missed the gum-smacking girl who used to work for him, but in the three months since Brenda left Jasper Gulch for the lure of the big city and better job prospects, his filing system had gone from bad to worse.

It had been a long, hot day, and it was only 9:00 a.m. The drought wasn't helping anyone's temper, least of all his. One of the area ranchers had called around four that morning because a cow was in labor and the calf was coming breech. Luke had gone straight out there, bleary-eyed and unshaven, and hadn't stopped since.

"Okay, Butch," he said. "I'm due out at the Anderson ranch in a few minutes. I'll stop at your place on my way by."

As he hung up the phone, his elbow hooked a stack of folders, sending an avalanche of papers to the floor. He grabbed for them, missed, dropped his bag to the desk and muttered one short, succinct word befitting his mood.

A sound near the door drew his gaze.

"Excuse me. I was wondering..." A woman he'd never seen before stood in the doorway.

Even in her loose-fitting shorts and tank top, she looked tired and warm, but these days who didn't? She had blue eyes, a mid-Western accent and, as far as he was concerned, universal appeal. Her hair might have been a little too red to be considered classically beautiful. It just so happened that red was his favorite color.

"Are you here about the ad?" he asked.

She turned her head toward him and studied him before answering. "Yes, I suppose I am."

If Luke Carson had been a man prone to smiles, a grin the size of South Dakota would have spread across his face right then. Glancing at her fingers, which were long and tapered and bore no wedding ring, he asked, "Can you do bookkeeping?"

Her eyes narrowed slightly. "Well, yes."

"What about filing?"

"Filing?"

"Can you do it?"

"Alphabetically? Numerically? Or by subject?"

It was all he could do to keep from raising his face and letting loose a yowling yee-ha. He didn't even bother to scowl when the phone started to ring again.

"How soon can you start?"

She opened her mouth to speak then closed it.

"Look," he said, glancing at his cluttered office. "I know how this must look, but there really is a method to this madness. We're in the middle of a drought out here, and the only other vet is more than a hundred miles away. The cattle are getting rangy, the horses are jumpy, and the area ranchers and cowboys are wound up tighter than a whirlwind in May. But I pay well, and I'll take whatever hours you can give me."

He turned up his famous Carson charm, pulling at the brim of hat and looking intently at her. "What do you say?"

He felt her eyes on him, liking the way her gaze trailed over his face, down the column of his throat all the way to the toes of his scuffed cowboy boots. He liked it even more when she finally walked into the room.

She took her time turning around, her shirt and hair settling into place with a quiet swish. Making a show of reading his name on his vet certificate on the wall, she said, "I think I could work mornings for a while, at least. When would you want me to start?"

His heart thudded, and his breath caught in his throat. "How does yesterday sound?"

The smile she gave him went straight to his head, but when she laughed out loud, every male hormone in his body came to life.

"I guess I'll see you tomorrow morning," she said. "About eight o'clock?"

"Eight o'clock sounds good."

"By the way, my name's Jillian Daniels. Oh, there's one more thing. Is that silver pickup truck outside yours?"

Luke nodded.

"Your lights are on."

A split second later, she was gone. And Luke was left

staring at the empty doorway of his cluttered veterinarian's office on the end of Main Street.

He couldn't remember the last time he'd reacted so strongly and so immediately to a woman he'd just met. He couldn't remember the last time it had felt so good.

Luke came out of his musings with a start. Striding outside, he turned off his lights then released a long breath. It was hotter than blazes out here. He'd grown up here in South Dakota and was accustomed to the high summer temperatures. But this summer was different. The sun shining overhead was merciless. It was going to be another scorcher; as usual, there wasn't a cloud in sight.

He spotted Jillian Daniels on the other side of the street, and suddenly the heat and dry weather didn't seem so bleak. There was a new woman in town, a woman with red hair and long legs and the softest blue eyes he'd ever seen.

Luke Carson's day had just gotten a whole lot better.

"It's been a month, a whole month!" Boomer Brown yelled from the back of the room. "And the only women who've moved to Jasper Gulch have brought their husbands and kids with them."

"Yeah!" another local shouted. "I thought you boys said that advertisement would bring *single* women to our corner of South Dakota."

Luke eyed the crowd that had gathered for tonight's town meeting, vowing to set these men straight as soon as he could get a word in edgewise, which, from the looks and sound of things, was going to be a while.

The sparsely furnished back room of Mel's Diner was practically bursting at the seams with about thirty ranchers and cowboys and rodeo riders who'd grown weary of the long, lonely nights they faced due to the shortage of women in the area. He'd never seen so many people turn out for one of these meetings, but then, none of them had ever had so much at stake before.

It *had* been a month since the *Jasper Review* reported the comments Luke's brother, Clayt, had made at the last meeting. It had been his idea to advertise for women to come to their town. Before anyone knew how it had happened, several big newspapers had picked up the story, coyly referring to Jasper Gulch as Bachelor Gulch. In the ensuing weeks, scores of women had come to check out the Jasper Gents. Unfortunately most of them had taken one look at the meager stores, the limited job prospects and dusty roads, and kept right on going.

It looked as if one, at least, had decided to stay. *Jillian Daniels.* Her name conjured up hazy images, while the memory of the smile she'd given him in his office that morning turned those images into an energy he had a hard time hiding.

It took incredible concentration to bring his attention back to the meeting. Isabell Pruitt, the self-appointed leader of the Ladies Aid Society declared, "I told you nothing good would come of this. If that advertisement draws anybody, it'll be harlots, women of ill repute, I tell you."

Every man in the room groaned out loud, which only made Isabell rise to her feet self-righteously and say, "Is that what you want? Is it? If it is, let the record state that I want no part of it. None whatsoever. And another thing…"

"Oh, put a sock in it, Isabell," one of the men groused.

Isabell pursed her thin lips and gave an affronted huff. "Well, I never!"

"Yeah? Maybe you should."

The argument that broke out between the members of the Ladies Aid Society and everyone else in the room was loud enough to bring down the roof. Luke swore under his breath and stood. Glancing to his right, he found that the

other members of the town council—Clayt, Wyatt Mc-
Cully, and old Doc Masey—had all risen, too.

During a momentary lull, Luke said, "Now, Isabell, we
went over this last month when I looked in on Sylvester.
How is that old mouser, anyway?"

Thankfully, nobody sputtered that the only thing wrong
with that cat was old age, and Isabell nodded stiffly before
sitting back down. Luke took advantage of the opportunity
to continue.

"Twenty years ago there were more than seven hundred
people living in the village of Jasper Gulch and outlying
areas. Today the number barely reaches five hundred."

"We lose more of our women every year," Doc Masey
added. "Not one girl in this year's graduating class is planning to stay in Jasper Gulch come fall. There are already
sixty-two bachelors, and it's only going to get worse. We
need more women in this town if we want it to survive for
future generations."

Wyatt's grandfather, Cletus McCully, snapped his suspenders and said, "We need more women if there are going to *be* future generations."

A couple of his old cronies snickered into their hands,
and Isabell's face turned red all the way to the roots of
her springy gray hair. The few people who were opposed
to the idea of bringing strangers into their quiet town continued to bicker with everyone else. Luke exchanged a
look with Clayt and Wyatt, then slowly sank back into his
folding chair.

He called for order. Then called again. The third try was
the charm, or at least as close to it as he'd likely see that
night, because with it, the men and women of Jasper Gulch
lowered their grumbling to a dull roar.

Very little air was moving through the open windows
at his back, and the native bachelors were getting restless.
Not that it wasn't perfectly understandable. The drought
was the worst they'd seen in twenty-two years. Jasper

Gulch needed a nice long rain and several dozen single women.

Luke only needed one.

He doubted that anybody had noticed anything different about him lately. His hair was still brown, his eyes were still gray, his frame the same lanky six foot two it had been since his seventeenth birthday. Aside from a few squint lines around his eyes, he didn't look much different from the way he had ten years ago when he was twenty-five. But it wasn't his appearance that was changing. It was as if a need had been sparked in the very center of him. It was the need for a woman, a special woman. He'd almost given up any hope of finding her. Now the possibilities seemed limitless.

The meeting progressed in a haphazard fashion. He, Wyatt, Clayt and old Doc Masey did their best to keep things under control, but it wasn't easy. The room grew hotter by the minute, and so did everyone's tempers.

"Do you have any idea how long it's been since somebody put a quarter in the jukebox in my bar?" DoraLee Sullivan complained.

"We might play poker at the Crazy Horse every chance we get," one of DoraLee's regulars grumbled, "but we draw the line at dancin' with each other. No sirree, Bob."

"See?" DoraLee insisted. "You boys have gotta do something to bring other women to Jasper Gulch."

"We're trying, but we all have to be patient," Clayt declared.

Jason Tucker, who worked for Clayt on the Carson family ranch just outside of town, sprang to his feet. "Patient? You expect us to be patient? Do you know how long it's been since one of us has had a date?"

Wyatt, the county sheriff, rubbed his chin and said, "Let's see. What year is this?"

Everyone chuckled, and Luke breathed his first easy breath since opening the meeting half an hour ago.

"Clayt's right," he declared. "We all have to be patient. That advertisement's working. New people are arriving every week. We all know we need new blood in our town. We also need plumbers and electricians and builders and bankers and just about everything else there is."

"The only things we don't need are more bachelors," Boomer Brown grumbled.

Luke opened his mouth to speak. "The single women will come. In fact…"

Cletus McCully cut in before he could finish. "I heard that one of those married couples you mentioned is planning to open a plumbing shop, and one of the other families has a daughter who wants to be a doctor someday, which brings me to the point I wanna make—"

"Nobody takes longer to make a point than you," Karl Hanson complained.

"You can say that again," someone else agreed.

"Do you boys wanna deface my character or do you wanna hear my idea?"

"Oh, all right," Karl said. "Let's hear what you have to say. But get on with it. It's hotter than blazes in here."

Grinning like the proverbial Cheshire cat, wrinkled though he might be, Cletus said, "I make a motion that we throw out the welcome mat to the newcomers of Jasper Gulch."

"The welcome mat?" Luke asked.

"That's right. The welcome mat. I'm thinking a town picnic would be in order here. We could even set up a dance floor and hire a country-western band."

"A dance floor!" one of the many bachelors groused.

"Cletus, are you crazy?"

"Who in the world are we gonna dance with? Married women?"

"See what I mean?" Isabell sputtered. "Only ill will come of this, I tell you."

Just when Luke was sure he'd never gain control of the

meeting again, the door leading to the diner opened. A low murmur went through the crowd as Wyatt's younger sister, Mel McCully walked in. As if on cue, everyone went perfectly still.

Mel wasn't alone.

Two women, one with dark hair, the other with red, slowly made their way to the center of the room.

"Well, looky here," Jason declared, looking for all the world like a yearling who'd seen his first female. "Women."

"Pretty ones, too."

"I'll be gol-darned."

Luke had never seen so many cowboy hats pushed higher off so many foreheads in so short a time. Mel stayed where she was near the back of the room, but the other two women slowly zigzagged toward the front.

"I do believe our prayers are being answered," Karl Hanson said.

Luke wondered how long Karl could hold his breath and suck in his belly at the same time. The dark-haired woman in front cast a covert glance all around and favored them all with a smile. The second woman turned her head, the overhead bulbs creating golden-red highlights in her hair. Luke's own stomach muscles tightened, but for an entirely different reason. His eyes narrowed, and a slow heat that had nothing to do with the sweltering temperatures shimmered through him.

He leaned back in his chair. And waited. For what, he wasn't sure. Maybe for the beating rhythm of his heart to return to normal. Or maybe to see if Jillian Daniels felt the same spark of attraction he did.

With a wink that turned young Jason Tucker's face three shades of red, the dark-haired woman said, "I'm Lisa Markman, and this is my friend, Jillian Daniels. We just moved into town this morning, and we were hoping you wouldn't mind answering a few questions."

"You can ask us anything, anything at all," Karl declared.

All the men chuckled, all except Luke. Lisa was talking about the family clothing store she planned to open, but Luke hardly heard. He was too busy watching Jillian. She'd changed her clothes since this morning. Now the skirt she wore was one of those trendy wraparound numbers he'd seen on TV—hip-hugging, calf-skimming, a fantasy in the making. He wasn't sure what it was made of, but the color was a deep, deep green. Her blouse was simple in design, sleeveless, scoop-necked and a rich shade of gold.

The other woman held up a stack of flyers and said, "I've done a lot of research since I saw your advertisement in the Madison papers, and I've listed some of the clothing I thought you might want me to stock. I'm going to start with the basics for now and expand as time goes on. I've rented the vacant store next door, and I've already talked to suppliers and wholesalers. If I pick up the merchandise myself, I should be in business in a week. That's where all of you come in. If you'd fill out one of these questionnaires and spread the word to your friends and neighbors, I'd really appreciate it."

Luke thought about the way Jillian had hesitated that morning when he'd asked if she had come about the ad. He'd been referring to his help wanted ad, but she'd obviously thought he'd meant the advertisement luring women to their corner of South Dakota.

She'd really only come in to tell him his lights were on. And yet she'd taken the job. Under the circumstances he wouldn't have blamed her if she'd taken one look at his ramshackle office and hightailed it out of there. But damn, he was glad she hadn't.

"What do you want us to do with the questionnaires when we're through?" Boomer asked.

Lisa answered, "You can either hand them to me tonight or bring them to the store. Or, if you'd rather, you can drop them in the mail. Our post office box is number 113. I always thought thirteen was unlucky, but Jillian has assured me that the way the moon and planets are aligned right now, it's very lucky, indeed.''

Luke watched as the women separated and began passing out flyers. He didn't know much about the alignment of the moon and planets, but there must have been something to this luck thing, because today felt like his lucky day.

Jillian worked her way around the crooked rows of chairs, handing a flyer to each man she passed. Within minutes she reached the front of the room where she held out a sheet of paper to Doc Masey and smiled at his friendly greeting. Clayt was next. And then Wyatt.

The only man left was Luke.

He took a deep breath. And waited. With her next step he could hear the soft rustle of her skirt. A rousing dose of anticipation played along his spine. She glanced at the stack of flyers in her hand and then straight into his eyes.

There was an instant parting of her lips and a slight lift of her eyebrows. She hesitated for a moment, then smiled at him the way she had earlier. Now he understood the knowing glint in her eyes. Holding up an old newspaper containing the town's advertisement for women, he asked, ''Why didn't you tell me you were here about *this* ad?''

Her lips curved upward the tiniest bit. In a voice barely loud enough to hear, she said, ''I knew you'd figure it out. Do you still need me?''

''You have no idea how much.''

Jillian Daniels couldn't feel her feet. That's how far her head was in the clouds. For a moment she was afraid that the delicate thread that seemed to have formed between her gaze and Luke Carson's was the only thing keeping her from floating completely away.

The man was more sure of himself and his masculine

appeal than she would have liked, but she could see why. He was tall, even sitting down. He looked more like a cowboy than the town vet. His jeans and shirt were faded, his shoulders broad, his skin tan. His hair was dark brown and in need of a trim. She wasn't sure if that was what gave him that roguish quality, or if it was the way he grasped the black hat resting on his knee.

There was something about him that seemed familiar. She'd noticed it that morning. Studying his face feature by feature, she couldn't recall having ever met him. And yet the sense of familiarity remained.

She swallowed with difficulty, then somehow managed to turn around again, finally breaking eye contact. It took her to the count of ten to get her breathing under control. It took even longer to reel in her thoughts. Fanning herself with the leftover flyers, she tried to put her thoughts in order, but that wasn't easy. Luke Carson was not an easy man to put out of her mind.

Lisa was talking on the other side of the room, and Jillian did her best to follow along. After all, helping Lisa get settled was what she was here to do.

"Does everyone have a questionnaire?" Lisa asked.

Several men held up their light blue sheets of paper. The rest all made agreeable sounds of one sort or another.

"Do you have any questions?" Lisa asked.

"I have one," a man nearly hidden in the very back of the room called. "Why isn't there any place on this form for my phone number?"

"Forget about your phone number, Karl," the stocky man sitting next to him said. "I'd rather know *their* telephone numbers. You gals are single, aren't you?"

Lisa's laugh was deep and throaty. Jillian had a feeling that more than one of these men would hear it in his dreams tonight. Waggling one finger, Lisa said, "I was sure your ad said you Jasper Gents were *shy*."

"Shy but willing," someone called.

"Now, are you gonna answer our question?"

Jillian met Lisa's gaze over the tops of more than a dozen cowboy hats. They shared a shrug and a mild shake of their heads before Lisa said, "Yes, it just so happens that Jillian and I are both as single as a long-stemmed rose. Now, we don't want to keep you from your meeting, so we'll be going. It was nice meeting all of you. Stop in at the store and see us real soon, ya hear?"

"Oh, we'll be there."

"You can count on it."

"You got that right."

"Yes sirree, Bob."

Watching Jillian and Lisa leave, Luke couldn't help noticing how well the two women communicated with just a look or a gesture. He wondered how long they'd been friends and had to fight the almost overwhelming desire to follow them out the door. Holding on to his composure, he tipped his chair back and hitched one boot over the opposite knee, calculating his next move.

"Cletus McCully, you old dog," Karl declared. "You were right, absolutely right."

"That's what I've been trying to tell you."

"Lisa and Jillian," someone said reverently. "Those are fine names, don'tcha think?"

"I wouldn't care if their names were Myrnella and Peerpont. They're fine looking," someone else declared.

"My mother's new furniture is fine looking. Lisa and Jillian are gorgeous," Jason insisted.

"And single."

"Yeah, single."

The front legs of Luke's chair met the floor with a definite click.

"How old would you say they are?" Jason asked.

"Who cares?"

"Yeah, who cares."

"Now about this welcome mat Cletus mentioned," Doc Masey began.

"A town picnic is a great idea," Karl said.

"With dancing?" Jason asked.

"Yep."

"With real live women and everything?"

"Yep."

"I second Cletus's motion!" Jason exclaimed.

"I third it."

"I fourth it."

"Everyone in favor, say aye!" Jason shouted.

The room echoed with a chorus of ayes. Before Luke, who was supposed to be running the meeting, could ask for any nays, Cletus said, "It looks like we're going to have us a town picnic."

A cheer went around the room. Cletus stood up and said, "Wyatt? You, Clayt and Luke can work out the details, can't you?"

"The details?" Wyatt croaked.

"Sure. I'll bet the kind women of the Ladies Aid Society would help you with the food. Isn't that right, Isabell? Meanwhile, we'll all spread the word. Seems to me there won't be much left for you three boys to do. Don't dilly-dally with your plans. The sooner we have the picnic the better."

"Now just a cotton-picking minute," Clayt grumbled.

Before Luke and Wyatt could add to Clayt's rebuke, someone who had no authority whatsoever moved to adjourn. Within seconds, men whose scowls had been miraculously replaced with wide grins nearly tripped over each other in their haste to be the first ones out the door. The next thing Luke knew, he, Wyatt and Clayt were alone in the sweltering room.

"It looks like we have a town picnic to plan," Wyatt said.

"What's worse, we have to ask Isabell Pruitt to help," Clayt grumbled.

"I could strangle my grandfather," Wyatt declared.

"I'd be glad to help," Clayt sputtered. "But I don't know how in the hell I'd fit it in."

Luke didn't think there was much he could add to that. After all, Clayt did have his hands full these days. It had only been a few weeks since his ex-wife had breezed into town just long enough to dump their nine-year-old daughter on his doorstep, saying that she'd had it with parenting. Haley might not have seemed like such a handful if Luke and Clayt's mother hadn't been called away to Oregon to care for her ailing mother, leaving her men to fend for themselves. The fact that the grass was burning up on the family spread only compounded Clayt's worries.

It took Luke a while to notice that nobody was talking. He looked from Clayt to Wyatt with 'What?' written all over his face.

Wyatt was studying Luke through narrowed eyes. "I was just wondering why you're not complaining louder than anybody about the fact that there are only two new women in town and sixty-two bachelors vying for their attention."

"That's right," Clayt cut in. "Why aren't you swearing up one side and down the other?"

Luke didn't think there was much use in trying to deny anything. After all, Clayt and Wyatt both knew him like the backs of their own hands. When he was good and ready, he hitched his fingers through his belt loops and rocked back on his heels.

"I don't particularly like the idea of competing with at least half the county for a woman's affections, but it just so happens that I have a little advantage."

"What advantage?" Clayt asked.

"It's not a big deal, really."

"Don't make me drag it out of you," Clayt threatened.

"Don't make me help him," Wyatt added.

Luke almost smiled.

"Well?" Clayt demanded.

Lowering his voice as if guarding a secret, Luke finally answered. "It just so happens that I know something the other bachelors don't."

"About the two new women?" Wyatt asked.

"About Jillian."

"I'll give you to the count of three," Clayt declared.

This time Luke didn't even try to keep the grin off his face. Glancing from Clayt to Wyatt, he said, "I know where she works."

"Where?" Two voices rose in unison.

"In my office. With me."

Clayt and Wyatt tipped their hats up at the same time, but Clayt was the first to find his voice. "How in Sam Hill did you manage that?"

With an unmistakable heat still vibrating through his body, Luke said, "Just my lucky day, I guess."

He turned around and, without another word, slowly sauntered out the door. Yes sirree. Today was definitely his lucky day. And from the looks of things, tomorrow was going to be even better.

Chapter Two

"Did you ever see so many cowboy hats in one room?" Jillian asked, looking up from the box of pots and pans she was unpacking.

"Forget the cowboy *hats,*" Lisa said coyly. "Did you ever see so many *cowboys* in one room?"

"This is ranching country, so it only stands to reason that there would be cowboys here."

Lisa pushed an empty box out of her way. With her hands on her hips she asked, "But doesn't it seem more than a little amazing how things are working out? I mean, what were the chances that we'd see that advertisement luring women to Jasper Gulch? Could it be possible that there really are men in the world who are looking for more than a one-night stand?"

"You heard what they said at the meeting tonight," Jillian answered. "The Jasper Gents are shy but willing."

"I think they might have been stretching the truth a bit with that *shy* part." Lifting her hair off her neck, Lisa asked, "Does it feel awfully warm in this kitchen to you?"

Jillian shook her head and said, "Do you think the fact

that you decided to stir up a loaf of cinnamon swirl coffee cake, which you baked in a kitchen that was already sweltering hot, has anything to do with that?''

Lisa shrugged. "I couldn't help it. After passing out those flyers to the people at the town meeting tonight, I had an incredible amount of restless energy. And you know I always cook when that happens.''

Straightening, Jillian strode to the refrigerator. Of course she knew that Lisa cooked when she got excited, just as Lisa knew that *she* couldn't boil water. Their knowledge of each other went back through a series of years, through a series of heartaches, of whispered secrets and treasured smiles, to a time when they'd both needed a friend more than they'd needed anything else in the world. In the face of such a friendship, the fact that they were complete opposites only made things more interesting.

"I've never felt like this before."

The deep, raspy note in Lisa's voice drew Jillian around. "What do you mean?"

"I've never felt on the verge of so many possibilities. I mean, just look at this kitchen. Look at this house."

Jillian glanced at the old-fashioned stove, the worn floor and painted cupboards. She'd seen a lot of kitchens that were more modern, but she knew what Lisa meant. This rented house marked a new beginning for Lisa, a chance at happiness, maybe even a chance at love.

Since the only items in the refrigerator were leftover burgers from a fast-food place in Western Minnesota and two half-empty cans of soda, she closed the door and stood leaning against it. A breeze wafted through the nearby screen, fluttering the flyaway wisps of hair around her face.

"You were lucky to find this house in so short a time."

Lisa muffled a yawn with one hand. "We can thank that sweet old Cletus McCully for that. I liked him the moment I met him when he showed us this house two weeks ago. He said he trusts me. Can you believe that? He didn't even ask for a security deposit. Did I tell you that he said people don't lock their doors at night in Jasper Gulch? I've never lived in a town like this, and I certainly never thought I ever would. But just look at us. We're here. You've already found a job, although I was hoping you'd take a little time off for a change, and I'm going to open a clothing store. Maybe you're right, Jillian. Maybe dreams really can come true.''

Jillian followed the course of Lisa's gaze out the window to the east. "Of course dreams really can come true. Travis and Cori are living proof.''

"Yeah. What do you suppose everyone's doing back in Wisconsin?" Lisa asked.

"They're probably doing what they always do at eleven-thirty on a week night. Sleeping.''

"I'll bet Travis and Cori aren't sleeping.''

Jillian shook her head at Lisa's reference to their friends who were planning to be married next month. "You, Lisa Markman, have a dirty mind.''

"That's what I've been trying to tell you for years.'' After a slight pause Lisa added, "Do you think they miss us?''

For at least the thousandth time since she'd met Lisa, Jillian wondered what it would take to make her friend see herself for what she really was. At five foot five, Lisa was a little shorter than Jillian. Her hair was thick and straight, the ends reaching to her shoulders, heavy tendrils brushing her eyebrows. On the outside was a woman who wore bright clothes, had a sultry laugh and a figure to die for, but inside she was one of the most caring and loyal people Jillian had ever known.

"Are you homesick, Lisa?''

"Who me?'' She straightened, visibly pulling herself together. "This is my home now. The Jasper Gulch Clothing Store is set to open in less than a week, and I've already met a good share of the bachelors here in town.''

A dozen men's smiling faces flashed through Jillian's mind, but only one *unsmiling* face remained. A strange kind of warmth started in her throat and slowly settled lower. Trying to think of something—anything—else, she said, "Did any of those men make a lasting impression on you?"

"I met so many of them in so short a time it's not easy to remember their names. Let's see. There was one man named Karl, and I think one of them said his name was Boomer. There was an Archie and a Ben and I remember a boy named Jason, and of course that sweet old Cletus McCully. And there was that woman named Mel who owns the diner and Isabell Pruitt, who, if you ask me, looks as if she makes a habit of sucking lemons, and I remember someone named Clayt."

"And Luke."

"Who?"

Jillian gave herself a mental shake. "Shouldn't the loaf of coffee cake be cool enough to eat by now?"

Lisa reached for a towel then hurried away toward the front door. Jillian stood perfectly still at the kitchen counter in Lisa's newly rented house. She could hear the sound her friend's bare feet made on the worn linoleum. Otherwise the night was silent.

She'd always heard that the plains were supposed to be windy places. Tonight only the barest of breezes wafted through the open window. She wondered what the weather was like in Wisconsin. Although her life in Madison hadn't been easy, it was still the one place in the whole world that she considered home. It was where she'd grown up, where her parents and grandparents were buried and where she'd met the three best friends she'd ever had. It had felt strange to leave Ivy Pennington and Cori Cassidy yesterday morning. But Cori was getting married soon, and Ivy, an older woman, who'd been the surrogate mother of them all, had encouraged Lisa and Jillian to check out the Jasper

Gents here in South Dakota. Lisa had been so excited about coming to Jasper Gulch, Jillian hadn't been able to turn down her request to come with her.

In all honesty she had been feeling at loose ends lately. And she *was* enjoying the change of pace. Her rent was paid on her apartment in Madison, and it was going to be fun to watch Lisa systematically search for the man of her dreams. But the one thing Jillian hadn't figured into her summer holiday agenda was her reaction to Luke Carson.

"Jillian," Lisa said, interrupting her train of thought, "where did you say you put that coffee cake?"

"Right there on the railing," she said, hurrying through the quiet house and out onto the porch. "Right there next to the..."

Her voice trailed away the moment she realized she was looking in the exact spot the loaf *should* have been. Walking to the edge of the porch, she checked the bushes then peered at the dark houses all around them.

"Someone must have taken it," she said incredulously.

"Someone stole our coffee cake?" Lisa whispered.

"It looks that way."

"Who in the world would steal such a thing at a quarter to midnight in the little town of Jasper Gulch?"

"Does it make you nervous?" Jillian asked, looking sideways at her friend.

Lisa's brown eyes lit up with excitement. "Are you kidding? We've only been in town for fifteen hours, and I've already had more fun than I had in an entire month in Madison. I wonder what other surprises are waiting for us in Jasper Gulch."

Luke Carson's image filtered through Jillian's mind all over again. She tried to blink it away.

Yawning again, Lisa said, "I'm about ready to fall asleep on my feet. If you want to go on up to bed, I'll turn out the lights."

Jillian looked at the dark houses all around, then at the

leaves that were stirring in the slight evening breeze. Keeping her voice as low as the murmur of insects hiding in the dry grass, she said, "You go ahead. I'll be in, in a little while."

"You aren't afraid to be out here by yourself after what happened to my cake?"

Jillian shook her head. She'd been on her own for a long time and knew how to take care of herself. Giving the dark windows of the neighboring houses a cursory glance, she said, "There's probably a perfectly logical explanation for that. Cletus McCully said that other than the ugly color of orange paint Bonnie Trumble used on the front of the Clip and Curl, the only crimes committed in Jasper Gulch are gossiping and jaywalking. So I doubt a hardened criminal stole our late-night snack. A stray dog probably took it, or maybe a raccoon. You go on ahead. I think I'll sit out here for a while and unwind."

Jillian sank to the top step and wrapped her arms around her knees, listening to the sounds Lisa made as she walked up the stairs. A short time later a pipe rumbled somewhere in the old house. And then the only sounds she heard were the squeaks of crickets and the wind in the eaves.

She sat there for a long time, the air slowly cooling her skin, the quiet slowly lulling her thoughts. When she'd agreed to accompany Lisa all these miles to Jasper Gulch, she'd wondered what she would do with herself. Just like that, she'd found a job. It had been completely unexpected, but not as unexpected as the longing she'd felt deep inside when she'd first looked into Luke Carson's eyes.

She tried to tell herself that the reason her longing was so unsettling was because it had come out of the blue. Surely it had nothing to do with the husky undertones in his voice or the intensity in his gray eyes. It wasn't as if she'd never experienced those feelings before. It was just that they had a way of leading straight to heartache. And Jillian didn't think she could survive any more of that.

She rose slowly and went inside, where she closed the doors and turned out the lights. She tiptoed up the stairs, washed her face and donned a clean nightgown. Crawling between the sheets, she stared at the moonlit shadows dancing on the dark ceiling, thinking about everything she'd done that day. She couldn't help wondering what tomorrow would bring.

She was certain of only two things. She was going to put an end to whatever it was she'd glimpsed in Luke Carson's eyes today and to whatever it was that had answered deep in her chest. And she was going to make sure he didn't get the wrong idea about her presence here in Jasper Gulch.

Yes, first thing tomorrow morning, that was what she was going to do.

"It looks as if you're making a dent in that stack of folders."

Jillian glanced over her shoulder and found her new employer leaning in the doorway. His arms were folded at his chest, his hat shading the upper part of his face. In the four hours she'd been there, he'd come and gone twice. She hadn't heard him return either time.

He'd met her at the door a few minutes before eight that morning and quickly filled her in on the operation of his small clinic, explaining that since this was cattle country he did most of his work out of his truck. He kept this small office here on Main Street to examine dogs and cats and an occasional hamster, but unless it was an emergency, he only scheduled appointments for every other Thursday. He'd pointed to the file cabinets, poked his head into his one-and-only examining room and had pretty much given her free rein of everything in between. Other than taking a few telephone calls, she'd spent the morning familiarizing herself with the workings of his practice.

"Are you getting a handle on Brenda's filing system?" he asked from the doorway.

Since she couldn't very well say something bad about someone she'd never met, she gave him a small nod and turned back to her filing.

"Liar."

Her double take didn't quite make him smile, but it raised his lips enough to crease one lean cheek. Pushing away from the doorjamb, he said, "Come on, Jillian. This is Jasper Gulch. If we didn't gossip, we'd have nothing to do. Everybody knows that the only way Brenda Townsend could figure out what letter came after *T* was to recite the entire alphabet from the beginning. So you don't have to try to protect her reputation."

She smiled to herself and reached for another stack of files. "Then it wouldn't be wrong of me to surmise that the gum stuck on the bottom of the chair belonged to your former office assistant?"

"You catch on fast."

She glanced at the name on the next file, wishing his simple compliment didn't make her feel so...complimented. Last night she'd vowed to set Luke straight about her presence in Jasper Gulch. It hadn't taken her long to realize that *that* was easier said than done. It wasn't that she hadn't tried. It was just that Luke Carson wasn't an easy man to deter. He had a restless energy that didn't permit him to stand in one place very long. She didn't know how a man his size did it, but he moved like lightning...without the thunder.

Reining in her thoughts, she asked, "Where did this Brenda go? When she left Jasper Gulch, I mean."

"To Sioux Falls. The girl hated to type, but she sure seemed to enjoy chasing me around the desk."

Being careful to keep her voice neutral, she said, "I would have thought it was the other way around."

He made a sound only men could manage and said,

"Give me some credit. The girl was nineteen and thought the olden days referred to the years before microwaves were invented. Believe me, I never chased Brenda Townsend around the desk, and I give you my word I won't chase you. But don't worry, I won't hold you to the same rule."

Jillian hadn't intended to turn around, but once she had, she couldn't look away. There was a maddening hint of arrogance about this man that was impossible to ignore. He might have been a country vet, but he was no country bumpkin. He had his masculine swagger down to an art form, and his smiles, well, they were just rare enough and just unexpected enough to chase nearly every coherent thought right out of her head.

Jillian stared wordlessly at him from her side of the cluttered old desk. He was watching her, his gaze steady, his expression thoughtful. His skin appeared even darker beneath his dusty black cowboy hat, his jaw square, his chin strong. As far as she was concerned, she'd noticed entirely too much about him. In fact, the first thing she'd done when she'd stepped foot inside the office that morning was notice he'd shaved. The second thing she'd done was give herself a mental kick for noticing in the first place. She gave herself another one, this time keeping her expression under stern restraint.

"Trust me, Luke. You have nothing to fear."

"Do I look afraid, Jillian?"

She fought against the urge to smile and lost. Tipping her head ever so slightly, she said, "I think you know exactly how you look."

"And how is that?"

She thought about all the words she could have used to describe him, but ended up shaking her head and saying nothing.

"Spoilsport."

A strange sensation of déjà vu washed over her. The

same thing had happened yesterday. Studying him intently, she said, "Have you ever been to a little town in Wisconsin called Maple Bluff?"

"No, I can't honestly say that I have."

"How about the University of Wisconsin? Have you ever been there?"

He took a step closer and shook his head. "I studied veterinary medicine at Michigan State, why?"

"It's nothing, really. I just can't shake the feeling that I've seen you someplace before."

Stopping on the other side of his desk, he said, "We've never met."

"How can you be so sure?"

"Because if we had, I'd remember. And so would you."

He didn't move, not even when the telephone started to ring. For a long moment neither did she. She thought she'd been prepared for the advances of the bachelors in Jasper Gulch. After all, it stood to reason that men who'd advertised for women would be interested in pursuing the new women in town. But she hadn't been prepared for Luke Carson's straightforwardness or his persistence. Actually she hadn't been prepared for anything concerning this man, least of all her instinctive response to him. Truth be told, she was strangely flattered by his interest. But Jillian couldn't afford to be distracted by romantic notions. Since she had no intention of leading him on, she knew she had to put an end to these feelings arcing between them once and for all.

By the time the telephone had jangled four times, she'd managed to gather her thoughts enough to ask, "Do you want me to answer that?"

He shook his head and reached for the receiver. With his voice a low drone in the background, she took another deep breath and turned back to her task. By the time he hung up the phone, she was well on her way to getting back on an even keel. "Another emergency?" she asked conversationally.

She felt his eyes on her back, but she didn't turn around.

"I guess you could say that, but not the way you mean. That was my brother, Clayt. I'm still not sure how it happened, but he, Wyatt McCully and I somehow managed to get ourselves roped into planning the town picnic. We put our heads together at the Crazy Horse last night, but I'm afraid we didn't get very far. DoraLee Sullivan, the owner of the Crazy Horse, said it was like watching three nuns plan a stag party."

Smiling at the mental picture his words evoked, she took her first casual breath since she'd found him lounging in the doorway several minutes ago. "Is the Crazy Horse the local saloon?"

"The one and only."

Keeping her eyes focused on the filing cabinet, she said, "Is that where the people of Jasper Gulch go for fun?"

"Aside from rolling up the sidewalks at eight every night, there isn't much to do in Jasper Gulch. Every now and then I mosey on down to the Crazy Horse to watch the old-timers play poker or listen to the local bachelors complain about the weather and the long, lonely nights out here."

Jillian couldn't imagine Luke Carson *moseying* anywhere, but she didn't think it would be wise to mention that particular observation *or* to ask about those long, lonely nights he'd mentioned, so she remained quiet. Unfortunately her stack of files had run out and so had her diversions. As if he knew it, Luke said, "There's been a noted lack of women in these parts lately, you know."

She turned around, smiling in spite of herself. "So I've heard."

"Have you also heard that things are starting to look up around here?"

Jillian wanted to believe he wasn't referring to her arrival in town, but the tone of his voice left little room for such possibilities. He was a decent man, and probably a lonely one. She wanted to warn him not to get his hopes up where she was concerned. More than anything she wanted to let him down easy, but how?

"I'd be happy to show you around the Crazy Horse sometime, Jillian. What are you doing tonight?"

He tipped his hat up, and for the first time since he'd stepped foot back inside the office, she saw the expression in his gray eyes. A zing went through her, and although she tried, she couldn't look away.

Luke didn't know what was going through Jillian's mind, but he knew what was going through his body. Damn, it felt good. He had half a mind to stride to the other side of the desk and reach for her hand, slowly drawing her closer, to tip her face up a little and gently cover her lips with his.

He took a step closer and then another. Before his eyes the expression in hers changed. Slowly, deliberately, she pulled her gaze away and turned her back on him.

Luke's footsteps froze in mid-stride.

He settled his hands on his hips, disappointed. What was going on here?

It didn't take long for his disappointment to make way for his anger. For crying out loud, this was the third time he'd brought up the subject of spending time with Jillian. And the third time she'd ignored him completely. He'd given her a few hours to feel comfortable, then had started hinting for a date. He hadn't thought too much of it when she'd given him a noncommittal hum when he'd suggested they catch a bite to eat in Pierre or take in a movie. At the time he'd assumed she hadn't heard. After all, she was up to her elbows in a new job. Now that he thought about it, she hadn't had any trouble answering his questions concerning her trip out here from Madison. And she hadn't given him that little hum when he'd told her how his great-

great-great grandfather, Jasper Carson, had come to found this town. Only his requests to spend time with her *outside* the office had been met with complete silence.

She'd heard his invitations. All three times. But she was ignoring them. Luke wanted to know why.

Keeping his voice purposefully low, he asked, "Ever been to the rodeo, Jillian?"

She shook her head cautiously. And Luke moved in to set the hook.

"That's too bad. The rodeo is South Dakota's number-one spectator sport. I don't think there's a living soul out here who doesn't look forward to rodeo days. Since I'd really hate to see you miss it, I'd be happy to take you."

Jillian didn't know where to look. She'd gone through the stack of files on the corner of the desk, so she couldn't look there. She half wished the phone would ring. But it didn't, and she couldn't look there, either. In the end she squared off opposite Luke and raised her gaze to his. The moment of truth wasn't far away.

"When do rodeo days begin?" she asked.

"In August."

"That's next month."

Although Luke raised his eyebrows, he didn't say anything. She felt like an idiot, anyway. He'd as good as told her he thought his former secretary didn't have both oars in the water, and here *she* was sounding even worse. It required all her willpower to hold his gaze, all her courage to say, "I appreciate your invitation, Luke, but I really can't make that kind of commitment."

"You can't."

Those two little words were issued in a clipped tone of voice men everywhere used moments before their patience went right through the roof. Giving her head a firm shake, she said, "No, I can't."

"Why the hell not?"

"Because," she said, keeping her voice as steady as possible. "I can't guarantee I'll still be here by then."

She closed her eyes, waiting for the explosion. When it didn't come, she chanced a glance his way. His lips were set in a firm line, his chest puffed out like a porcupine's quills. She quickly diverted her gaze to her watch. "Would you look at the time! It's twelve o'clock already, and I told Lisa I'd help her in the store right after lunch."

Without another word, she hurried to the back room where she'd stashed her purse first thing that morning. When she came out again, she couldn't help noticing that Luke hadn't moved an inch. It was the longest she'd seen him stay in one place all morning.

"Well," she called over her shoulder. "I'll see you tomorrow. Eight o'clock sharp. 'Bye."

The blast of hot air from the street brought Luke out of his stupor. He didn't know what was happening to his concentration, but he didn't like what had just happened to his ego. He'd asked Jillian out four times, which was exactly how often he'd been shot down.

He scooped his hat off his head with one hand and rubbed his face with the other. The Carson brothers may not have had much in the patience department, but they'd never had any trouble with women. Luke himself had turned a fair number of heads in his day, even with the lack of females in the area these past few years. Until about a minute ago he'd been confident that he could turn Jillian's.

What the hell did she mean she couldn't guarantee she'd be here next month? Where was she planning to go? He supposed he could wait until she came to work in the morning to find out. Wait, hell.

He crammed his hat back on his head and strode straight out to the sidewalk. He didn't even bother to close the door.

It was high noon, and some of the people of Jasper Gulch were out and about. Cletus McCully was sitting in his usual spot on the bench in front of the post office, and Opal Graham and her spinster daughter Louetta were heading for the diner for their usual Tuesday lunch.

Luke spotted Jillian trying to cross the street in front of Josie's Five and Dime. Shading her eyes with her hand, she glanced to the right and then to the left, waiting for Karl Hanson to move his old truck on down the street. Luke headed toward her, his long strides eating up the sidewalk in record time. By the time she stepped off the curb, he was only five yards away.

"Jillian, wait!"

She looked over her shoulder and came to an abrupt stop.

He slowed his steps and called, "You need a key."

"A what?"

He took another step, feeling the heat rise off the pavement in waves. "A key. I never know when I'll have to make an emergency run to one of the ranches. If it happens in the middle of the night or early in the morning, I can't guarantee I'll be able to open the office at eight."

"Oh, in that case..."

Jillian's lips continued to move, but an approaching car in dire need of a new muffler drowned out whatever else she was saying. From the corner of his eye, he saw a rusty splotch of brown and fleetingly wondered why Roy Everts didn't break down and get that car of his fixed. The old man drove like a maniac, taking out fence posts and mailboxes every other day. Luke turned his head just in time to see Roy take the corner wide, barreling through the town's only stop sign. In a flash Luke realized the old geezer was about to take out Jillian today.

"Jillian. Look out!" Luke reached her on the run, his feet moving before his brain had decided what to do. A horn blared just as his arm snaked around her waist. He pulled her to his chest so hard it knocked the wind out of her.

Roy missed her by two feet.

Craning her neck to look at the car, which had come to a stop in front of the Crazy Horse, she gasped, "Who was that?"

Another time Luke would have called Roy every name in the book. But right that minute all his concentration was fixed on the woman in his arms. He'd noticed she was slender the first time he'd seen her, but he'd had no way of knowing how soft and pliant she would feel in his arms. Her hair smelled of warm flowers, her white blouse a thin barrier between his callused hand and the soft skin at her waist. This close, her eyes were an even lighter shade of blue and were wide open, staring into his.

"His name is Roy. Don't worry, Cletus is already giving him the tongue lashing he deserves. Not that it'll do any good."

She moved, her thigh brushing his, her breathing expanding her chest, which in turn expanded his. Her lips were parted slightly and so full he was tempted to kiss her, here and now.

"Luke, what are you doing?"

Her voice was a husky rasp, but it brought him to his senses. He wouldn't have minded kissing her in the middle of Main Street. But first kisses were meant to be private, especially if they were going to lead to second kisses.

Loosening his hold on her, he said, "I'm saving your life, of course."

She glanced around. And stiffly stepped back. "Oh. I suppose you're right. Um. Well. I don't know what to say."

She sounded breathless. Luke didn't blame her. His breathing was still ragged, too. But his mind was functioning normally, and as far as he was concerned, there were several things she could say. She could tell him she'd be happy to go out with him, for starters. And maybe she could follow that up with an invitation of her own.

Unfortunately she didn't appear to be getting ready to say either of those things. She was looking decidedly ill at ease. Since he didn't want to scare her away, he tugged on her hand, drawing her with him to the curb.

Without releasing her fingers, he said, "Why don't you say you'll have lunch with me."

"Lunch?"

"Yes, lunch. Come on, Jillian. I just saved your life. In some cultures that would make you mine."

Her chin came up, and her hand stiffened in his. If Luke lived to be a hundred, he doubted he would ever see a more serious expression on another person's face. He felt his own eyes narrow and his adrenaline kick into over-drive, because he recognized the look of a woman gearing up to speak her mind.

Chapter Three

Jillian tried not to bristle as she shot a quick glance at the people who were out and about on the narrow main street. She could hear Cletus McCully's rusty old voice a half block away and an occasional grumble from the man who'd nearly run her down. Two women were standing beneath the diner's faded awning across the street, and a handful of men were watching from the shade next door.

She remembered Luke telling her how the people of Jasper Gulch liked to gossip and realized that he was still holding her hand. This wasn't the place she would have chosen to have this conversation, but she supposed saying what she had to say in front of the town's watchful eyes had its merit.

After a long pause she firmly, deliberately, pulled her hand from his. "You may have saved me from serious injury, Luke. But my life is very much my own."

He looked as if he would have liked to argue, but shrugged instead. "All right, Red. I can respect that. Now, how about that lunch?"

"My hair is *not* red." Jillian's mouth dropped open, his

slow grin sending the air whooshing out of her lungs. What did she care what color he called her hair? And why did it feel as if her heart was doing a pirouette inside her chest?

"Red, gold, brown and amber. It's beautiful. Now, do you want to stand here and argue or do you want to go inside Mel's Diner—where it's air-conditioned—and have lunch?"

For a full five seconds Jillian couldn't speak. Feeling inordinately warmed in ways she preferred not to examine, she crossed her arms, doing everything in her power to conquer her involuntary reaction to this man.

"I'm *not* having lunch with you, Luke."

"Aren't you hungry?"

She released a huff of air at the poor impression he did of looking innocent. "Yes. No. I mean, my hunger has nothing to do with it."

That got his attention. His eyes narrowed and he lowered his chin. "Would you care to explain what this *does* have to do with?"

Actually, she'd rather not, but didn't see any way around it. "Look, if I have lunch with you, people will get the wrong idea about us."

"And what idea is that?"

"They'll think we're a couple."

He no longer looked as if he was trying to appear innocent. The mixture of surprise and curiosity on his face was definitely the real thing.

Jillian took a deep breath. She was doing this badly. She couldn't blame Luke for jumping to conclusions. She had, after all, come to a town that had advertised for women, so it was no wonder he'd assumed she would be interested in dating the local bachelors.

Trying for a conciliatory tone of voice, she said, "I know this seems odd, but I didn't come to Jasper Gulch to find a man."

He made that sound again, the one a man makes when

he's holding on to his temper by a thread. His gray eyes darkened to the color of thunderclouds, and his voice dropped an entire octave as he said, "Let me get this straight. You saw the ad for Bachelor Gulch, so you moved here. But you aren't looking for a man."

"That's right."

"Then would you mind telling me why you're here?"

"I came to help Lisa get settled, and to help her find the man of her dreams."

"Lisa's looking for a man. But you aren't."

"Yes. No. I mean that's right. Lisa is, I'm not."

He didn't move a muscle, not even to blink. He was still looking at her incredulously, but all in all he'd taken that better than she'd expected.

Glancing at all the people who were watching this little interaction, she considered walking away without saying another word. She hated to do that to him. He'd given her a job and was a member of this town, had in fact been one of the people responsible for bringing new women to Jasper Gulch. How would it look to have one of those women stomp on his ego in front of more than a dozen residents?

She hadn't wanted the people of Jasper Gulch to get the wrong impression about her and Luke, but now she realized that as long as Luke understood, she didn't care what anyone else thought. His reputation and social standing were on the line here. It just so happened that she knew exactly what to do to save them.

With quiet assurance, she laid her hand on his forearm, reached up on tiptoe and whispered a kiss along his jaw. In a voice meant for his ears alone, she said, "This is for the people watching. I'm really not in the market, Luke, but believe me, if I was, you'd be a fine choice."

Without waiting for him to reply, she stepped back, turned on her heel and hurried across the street.

* * *

Luke came out of his befuddled state just as Jillian disappeared inside the new clothing store on the other side of the street. His arm felt warm where she'd touched him, and he swore he could still feel the gentle brush of her lips on his jaw.

She'd kissed him right here on Main Street in front of God and everyone. Not on the mouth. And not out of passion. She'd kissed him so he could save face.

It had worked. Cletus McCully and Roy Everts were both grinning from ear to ear while Opal and Louetta Graham whispered behind their hands. Even Ed, the town's only barber, was giving him a thumb's-up signal from beneath his red-and-white barber pole next door.

A slow heat that had nothing to do with the noon temperature washed over Luke, and his blood began to do a slow boil. He didn't want charity, and he damned well didn't need it.

He'd always prided himself on being somewhat of a lady's man. Somewhat, hell. He felt downright smug about his ability to ignite a woman's desire and expertly take her to great heights of pleasure. Sure there had been a noted lack of women out here these past few years, but he'd never had any trouble impressing the members of the opposite sex. He'd known his share of women in college and a few since. And not one of them had ever kissed him one second and told him she wasn't in the market the next.

The market?

He wasn't real estate, dammit.

He swallowed, hard, the set of his chin and the fury in his expression draining the grin from Cletus McCully's wrinkled face. Luke knew his sudden trek across the street was met with more than one pair of raised eyebrows, but frankly, he didn't care. He strode to the opposite curb and over the cracked sidewalk in front of the new clothing store. Without breaking stride, he gave the door a swift yank.

Several of the area bachelors looked up when he entered, but he didn't stop to chat. He didn't even bother saying hello. In fact, he didn't slow his pace until he came within a few feet of the red-haired woman who was poking through a carton near the back of the store.

He knew the instant Jillian noticed him. She turned to face him, folded her arms and settled her weight on one foot. Luke scowled all over again. If she thought her protective stance was going to hold him off, she could think again. He'd faced bigger, meaner, ornerier opponents than her—snorting bulls who didn't want an inoculation and stallions who didn't want to be corralled. Oh, no, he'd never let a little thing like a defiant glare stop him before, and he wasn't about to start now. He and Jillian were going to get something straight between them once and for all.

Jillian didn't know what was going through Luke's mind, but it couldn't have been pleasant. He'd planted himself in front of her, his feet spread apart, his hips thrust forward, his eyes never leaving her face. His lips were set in a straight line, his stare drilling her to the floor.

It wasn't easy to think when he turned all that roaring intensity on her, so she let her instincts guide her. And her instincts were telling her she'd sorely misjudged him.

"Luke, I..."

He held up one hand, and she stopped. He reached for her wrist, pulling her fingers from the crook of her right arm. Turning her palm toward the ceiling, he pressed a key into its center and curled her fist around it.

"I don't take charity, Jillian. And I don't give a rip what the people of this town think."

With a tug on the brim of his hat, he turned on his heel. He didn't utter another word. He didn't have to. The slamming of the door spoke volumes.

She stared into space, her mind blank, her heart racing. When the room finally came back into focus, she glanced around. The local bachelors who were helping Lisa in the store quickly averted their eyes and went back to work hanging shelves and unloading boxes. Lisa's attention wasn't so easy to divert. She tucked her hair behind her ears and quickly made her way to the back of the store.

In a voice barely above a whisper, she said, "What in the world was that all about?"

Jillian became aware of an ache in her hand and slowly opened her fingers. Tracing the indentation the key had made in her soft skin, she said, "That was my new boss, Luke Carson. He dropped off this key to the office."

"*That* was the local vet?"

Jillian nodded.

"You didn't tell me he was so good-looking. Or so tall."

Jillian glanced around the room. She didn't catch any of the bachelors in the act of looking at her, but several of them were paying a lot of attention to the toes of their scuffed cowboy boots.

She'd spent the first eleven years of her life in a small town, and knew how quickly gossip could spread. This little scene would no doubt be all over Jasper Gulch within the hour, which was exactly why she'd given Luke that kiss in the first place. She'd meant it to be a balm to his ego, but her plan had backfired. She'd tried to protect his reputation, to prevent the other men from knowing she'd turned him down. With very few words he'd let her know exactly how he felt about that.

Jillian wondered why his reaction to her little performance brought out airy hopes she'd forgotten she even had. Unfortunately, with that hope came a dark sense of gloom she understood all too well.

"So, do you have a thing for the local vet?"

Jillian almost choked on her next breath. "Lisa, for heaven's sake. You know I'm not going to stay in Jasper Gulch."

Lisa sighed, her smile a little sad. "I know, Jillian. I was just hoping you'd change your mind."

Biting down on her lip, Jillian felt herself going soft inside. "You've been one of my closest friends for fifteen years, and it sure isn't going to be easy to go back to Madison without you. But you know my stay here is only temporary. We both do."

Lisa took a deep breath and heaved a great sigh. Within moments a wry grin stole across her face. Inclining her head to the left, she said, "That might be true, but we're both here now, and on the other side of this very room are men who've been deprived of feminine companionship for far too long."

"Lisa, you're incorrigible."

"I know. You've gotta love me for it, don't you?"

Jillian shook her head, wondering how she'd ever gotten lucky enough to have met Lisa Markman all those years ago. Cori Cassidy and Ivy Pennington, too, for that matter. Life hadn't been easy for any of them back in Wisconsin, but one thing Jillian had learned from living these past thirty years was that she could face just about anything as long as she had friends at her side.

"Now come on," the most brazen and brassy of those friends said with a wink and a gentle nudge. "We have a captive audience, and I don't intend to waste it."

"Lisa, for heaven's sake. They'll hear you."

Lisa brushed the hair from her eyes and brought her chin up at a proud angle. She was wearing faded cutoffs and a T-shirt, but Jillian doubted she'd ever seen a more regal pose. Keeping her voice low and steady, Lisa said, "If one of these bachelors turns out to be the man for me, he's going to have to love me for who I am, what I am, the way I am."

Jillian nodded, wondering what there was about the air in this room that brought out so much pride and vigor in a person. It had been apparent in Luke's expression a few minutes ago and in Lisa's right now.

Maybe it wasn't the air in the room. Maybe it was the character in the people themselves.

Lisa strode to the front of the store where some of the local men were waiting to help in any way they could. Jillian stayed where she was, running the tip of one finger over the key in her hand, trying to figure out what, exactly, was different about the beating rhythm of her heart.

"It's up to you. We can do this the hard way. Or the easy way. But one way or another we're going to do it."

Luke rested his forearms along the narrow edge of the wooden fence behind Clayt's house, watching as his brother attempted to slip his boot into the stirrup on a year-and-a-half-old quarter horse. The filly appeared to have other ideas. She puffed out her chest and skittered to the side. As usual when greeted with opposition of any kind, Clayt dug in his heels and clenched his teeth.

Eyeing the horse's dark eyes and the obstinate tilt of her head, Luke said, "She looks awfully spirited, Clayt. Maybe you should train her from the ground for a few more weeks before trying to ride her."

Keeping his voice firm and steady, Clayt said, "I've tried. She's as open to ground training as she is to this. I'm going to ride her. Today."

"What's your hurry?"

Clayt took an ominous step closer to the animal. "Haley likes her. God only knows why. But this horse is the first thing that girl has taken an interest in, in the two weeks she's been here."

Luke adjusted the blade of prairie grass he was chewing on and hiked one foot onto the fence's lowest rung. So, his nine-year-old niece was finally starting to come around after being dumped so unceremoniously on Clayt's doorstep by his ex-wife. Luke knew that Clayt had been worried about the kid, and rightly so. Haley had been lethargic, and her appetite was almost nil. Under the circumstances, Luke supposed he couldn't blame his brother for wanting to break the horse for his little girl. And he wasn't really surprised the kid had chosen this particular animal for her own. When she wasn't sleeping, his freckle-faced niece was a pistol, and a Carson through and through.

But then, so was Clayt.

As if to prove it, Clayt hitched his boot into the stirrup and reached for the saddle horn. "All right, sister, here we go. Believe me, this is going to hurt me a lot more than it's going to hurt you."

He swung into the saddle like a pro, one hand in the air, the other loosely grasping the reins. The quarter horse snorted, tossing her head and kicking up her hind legs. Clayt landed on the packed ground with a loud thud and a string of cuss words that could have singed the grass just as surely as the hot sun overhead.

"Females," he sputtered.

Luke lifted the rim of his hat, his gaze straying to the cloud of dust his father was making as he sped away down the lane that divided Clayt's small parcel of land and the spread he worked with their father. Luke had exchanged a few words with Hugh Carson when he'd arrived ten minutes ago. His ears were still ringing from his father's reply. Looking back, he realized he should have known better than to inquire after his mother. After all, his father had several sore subjects. And these days, Rita Carson was the sorest of them all. All because she'd gone back to Oregon three weeks ago to help her sisters care for their ailing mother, leaving her poor, defenseless husband of thirty-seven years to fend for himself. In reality, Hugh Carson was about as defenseless as a mountain lion, but he'd been as spiteful as a wet hornet ever since.

Glancing from his father's cloud of dust to his brother's

cloudy expression, Luke said, "It looks as if the Carson luck has deserted all three of us today."

Clayt climbed to his feet and slapped the dust from his jeans with his hat. In a voice that sounded more like a growl, he said, "Don't tell me some female's dropped you on your rear end, too."

Remembering the way Jillian had kissed his cheek a few hours ago, and how she'd cleanly, neatly let him know that she wasn't planning to stay here in Jasper Gulch, Luke grimaced all over again. "You could say that."

Clayt crammed his hat back on his head, hobbled over to the fence and slowly climbed up. "The redhead?"

Luke didn't bother to nod.

"I thought you said you had a definite advantage where she was concerned."

Eyeing his only brother, Luke bit down on the blade of grass and joined Clayt on the top of the fence. The filly was keeping her distance in the shade of the barn. There were a few low outbuildings to the west. Beyond them was the Carson ranch, a rolling stretch of property that started two miles from the edge of town and stopped on the other side of Stoney Creek, which was fast turning into a narrow trickle. Most of the ranches around here ranged from two to five thousand acres, which was small compared to the seventy-five-thousand-acre spreads farther west. None of the men around here were getting rich, but in a good year most of them made enough to feed their families and put a little money away for a rainy day. Unfortunately it didn't look as if this was going to be one of those years.

"So? Do you have an advantage or don't you?" Clayt prodded.

"I thought I did."

"Then what's the problem?"

Giving his brother a sardonic glare, he said, "She said she isn't going to stay in Jasper Gulch."

"Did she say why?"

Luke's eyes narrowed slightly at the question. "As a matter of fact, she didn't."

"Maybe you should find out. And then maybe you should change her mind."

Clayt made it sound easy. Why wouldn't he? He hadn't been kissed out of pity. The thought still grated on Luke's nerves. He thought about pointing out the fact that his brother hadn't been able to talk his former wife into staying seven years ago, but didn't see much sense in dredging up old baggage. Keeping his gaze straight ahead, Luke said, "You never did tell me how Victoria was when she dropped Haley off."

Clayt made a sound deep in his throat and felt in his pockets for the pack of cigarettes he hadn't carried in more than five years. Patting his empty pocket, he said, "She was as beautiful and as selfish as she always was. I sure wish I'd have seen the selfish part when I first met her."

Luke didn't bother reminding Clayt that everybody smart enough to put two thoughts together had pointed it out in vivid detail when Clayt had first brought Victoria home ten years ago. There was a time when Luke and Clayt had fought like cats and dogs. Early in their teens, they'd both learned that although a raised fist could be a great stress reliever, it rarely took care of a problem. And Clayt Carson had plenty of those. The grass on the family ranch was burning up, and he suddenly found himself raising a daughter he hardly knew.

Staring across the corral, Luke said, "You know what they say, Clayt. Love is blind. Besides, if you'd have seen that side of Victoria, you wouldn't have Haley now."

"Yeah. And I plan to do right by that little kid if it takes me a hundred years."

"She could use a mother," Luke pointed out.

"What she wants is that horse." Without another word

Clayt climbed down from the fence and slowly made his way toward the dark brown filly.

"If you get back on that horse, you know darn well she'll just buck you off again," Luke called to Clayt's back.

"I'm a Carson." As if that said it all, Clayt shrugged one shoulder then set off for the other side of the corral.

Luke was vaguely aware that it took his brother a few minutes to catch the horse and that it only took the horse a few seconds to throw him off all over again, but the majority of his attention was turned inward where he was mulling over something Clayt had said. *I'm a Carson.* Luke was a Carson, too, which, among other things, meant that he was obstinate, ornery and as stubborn as the day was long. As far as Luke was concerned, that wasn't necessarily a bad thing. He was much too stubborn to give up on Jillian Daniels simply because she didn't happen to be looking for a man. After all, his mother always said the best treasure in the world was the one a person didn't even know he—or she—was looking for.

Sliding to the ground, Luke started off across the gravelly yard.

"Hey!" Clayt called. "Where are you going?"

Luke turned partway around. "I'm heading out to Forest Wilkie's place to immunize some calves."

Scooping his hat off the ground, Clayt said, "That doesn't explain why you suddenly got your swagger back."

"Who said I ever lost it?"

The horse snorted and so did Clayt. After a long pause he said, "That redhead had better watch out."

"She says her hair isn't red."

Clayt's laughter brought a slow grin to Luke's face. It was uncustomary for him to carry a smile around with him, but, striding to his truck, he realized that something uncustomary was happening inside him, too. It had all started when Jillian Daniels first stepped foot inside his office yesterday morning. There was something going on between them, something warm and vibrant and darned near irresistible.

Maybe Clayt was right. Maybe it was time he found out why Jillian wasn't planning to stay in Jasper Gulch. Once he knew what he was dealing with, he'd be able to determine just how to go about changing her mind.

Now all he needed was a little luck and a little time alone with one red-haired woman who *thought* she wasn't planning to stay in Jasper Gulch.

Luke threw the shift lever into park and ran a hand across the stubble on his chin. Getting a little time alone with Jillian was proving to be easier said than done. Two days had passed since he'd decided it was high time they got to know each other better. Now he realized he should have let the area animals in on his plan. Maybe then they would have cooperated.

A few days ago the cattle had needed his attention. Now it was the horses. He'd driven from one corner of his territory to the other, treating everything from thrush to lameness, with a birth for a first-time mother thrown in for good measure. It was this drought. It was making everyone crazy, animals included. What was worse, the whole situation was wreaking havoc with what little free time he had.

He'd just come from Pierre where he'd picked up a case of supplies. He'd taken longer than he'd planned to, but at least it was still morning, which meant that Jillian would still be in the office.

He took the box from the back of the truck and headed for his office door. He would have made it, too, if he hadn't come within a foot of running headlong into Cletus McCully. Criminy, he had lousy timing.

Luke knew darn well the old geezer saw him cringe.

That didn't stop Cletus from snapping his suspenders and saying, "It's a good thing for you I caught up with you when I did."

The sun was hot, and Luke's box of supplies grew heavier by the second. He shifted to one foot, then shifted to the other. Hiking the box higher into his arms, he said, "Cletus, I'd love to stay and talk, but there's someone I have to see."

A strangely knowing expression crossed Cletus's wrinkled face. Giving his suspenders another tug, he said, "That's what I wanna talk to you about. What do you think you're doin'? I saw the way that new gal kissed you the day before yesterday. Next thing I knew, you were stormin' out of the new store like a bat outta hell. It's all over town that you two already had a tiff. These boys are serious competition, Luke. They're moving in on her faster than a bear moves in on honey. Now here's what you gotta do."

Luke gave Cletus a sardonic look and took a backward step. The day he took advice about women from a seventy-nine-year-old man who'd been a widower for almost forty years was the day they might as well put him six feet under. Keeping his voice ominously low, he said, "I've got it under control, Cletus."

"That's what you think. Now listen up."

"Cletus, I mean it. I know what I'm doing."

The old man looked at him skeptically. "I just don't want you botching things up, that's all."

"I'm not going to botch anything up."

Cletus gave a loud harrumph, part of the sound coming from his throat, the rest escaping through his nose. "Fine. When you're ready to take my advice, you know where to find me. Just don't wait too long, ya hear?"

That said, he gave another affronted huff and ambled back to his bench underneath the shade tree in front of the post office. Luke was finally free to make his way toward his own office at the end of the street.

Before he could do more than jiggle the knob, Jillian opened the door from inside. She'd obviously been watching for his arrival.

This was more like it.

Luke puffed up his chest, wishing Cletus were here to see. Jillian made room for him to enter, and Luke squeezed past her, thoroughly enjoying the close quarters.

"Good morning," she said. "You have patients this morning."

He had half a mind to ask her how she managed to smell like a garden of flowers in the middle of the worst drought in more than twenty years. Instead, he sent her his best disarming half smile and said, "You must be mistaken. One thing we Carson's have never had is patience."

With a dawning look of realization, she glanced at him over her shoulder. "Not patience. Patients," she whispered. "As in dogs."

Dogs?

By the time Luke's eyes had adjusted to the dim interior, he was beginning to understand what Cletus had been trying to tell him. Boomer Brown was sitting on the corner of the desk. Ben Jacobs was leaning against the filing cabinet, and that young punk, Jason Tucker, was sitting in *his* chair.

"Mornin', Luke."

"Hey, Luke."

"Yeah, hey."

Luke cast each of them a narrow look. "Boys. What brings you here?"

Boomer pointed to his feet, where a big tan dog was snoring loudly. "Elmer here's been actin' kind of funny."

"Funny," Luke echoed.

"Yeah. You know. Sick."

Aside from the fact that the dog was twenty pounds

overweight and had already outlived his life expectancy, the old mutt looked perfectly healthy to Luke.

"Brutus has been under the weather, too," Ben declared, scratching his black lab behind the ears.

"Flash, too," Jason said.

If these dogs were sick, Luke would eat his hat. "Jason," he said, "I didn't know you had a dog."

"I haven't had him long," Jason answered, finally dragging his eyes from Jillian.

Long? Luke would bet his license the kid hadn't had him for more than a day. How obvious could these bachelors get?

Since there wasn't much he could do except examine the animals, he placed his box of supplies on the desk and removed his hat. "All right, boys, why don't you bring your dogs into the examining room, one at a time."

Jillian smiled at the three new patients in that soft way she had. Ben, Boomer and Jason exchanged a look, then smiled back. Luke wanted to bite glass.

He examined the puppy first and then Ben Jacobs's black lab. He didn't see much of Jillian, but every time her throaty laughter floated to his ears from the next room, his scowl deepened. She left before Boomer Brown could rouse his old dog from his nap. Luke only hoped Boomer hadn't had any better luck rousing her interest.

That man was getting on Luke's nerves. Boomer had been a couple of years ahead of him in school. Aside from being a little loud and obnoxious, Luke had always considered him a decent enough man. Suddenly he wished Boomer had been the one needing a shot instead of his dog. Luke had just the needle in mind.

By shortly after twelve o'clock, he'd administered three rabies shots—to the dogs, not their owners—had diagnosed two cases of fleas, one case of obesity and one case of dashed hopes where spending time alone with his new office assistant was concerned.

If he wasn't careful, he was going to have to break down and ask Cletus for advice. After sending the last patient on his way, he banished the thought, hoping to high heaven it would never come to that.

The doorknob rattled again. As if he'd had it planned all along, Cletus stepped into the room.

"Now are you ready to listen, boy?"

It was all Luke could do not to drop his head into his hands.

"Didn't I tell you those boys were gonna be serious competition? Now here's whatcha gotta do."

Luke eyed the door, then dropped into his worn desk chair. It looked as if he was going to have to listen to Cletus's advice whether he wanted it or not.

Chapter Four

Jillian dimmed the lamp next to her bed and slowly turned in a circle. She'd come up to her room with every intention of going to sleep. She supposed she was tired enough, but the thought of crawling into the big double bed didn't seem very appealing. Not that there was anything wrong with the bed. Like the entire house, the mattress was old but comfortable, her room pleasant in a well-used, old-fashioned kind of way. In fact, the faded wallpaper and furniture reminded her of her grandfather's house, where she'd lived for eight years. The room just didn't hold much appeal tonight.

Trailing her hand along the wall in the narrow hall, she meandered downstairs, the steps creaking beneath the smooth soles of her sandals. She sat in the wooden rocker, one of the few items she'd brought with her from Madison, and allowed the rocking motion to cease. Sitting in the quiet house, she thought about her apartment back home. Fleetingly she wondered if Allison, her friend Cori's sixteen-year-old daughter, had watered her plants. Jillian wasn't worried and realized that she wasn't so much homesick as she was lonesome. Lisa was out with one of the local bachelors. She'd invited Jillian along, but since the last thing Jillian wanted to do was come between Lisa and her search for Mr. Right, she'd declined.

She'd spent a good part of the evening tidying up the house and unpacking the remainder of her things. When she'd finished, she'd treated herself to a long, soothing shower. Now she was cool and comfortable, her hair was almost dry, the house was clean, and the night was much too quiet.

It wasn't like her to run out of things to do. Now that she thought about it, she wondered if this might be the first time it had happened in her entire life. Not that there weren't other things she could have done tonight. Melody McCully, who owned the local diner downtown, had issued a standing invitation to stop in anytime. Jillian had thought about it, she really had. Now she wished she'd gone.

The thought of Melody McCully brought to mind the peach pie the blond-haired woman had brought over earlier, welcoming Jillian and Lisa to Jasper Gulch. Jillian jumped to her feet and hurried into the kitchen, happy to have thought of something to do.

After sliding a generous slice onto one of the mismatched plates from the cupboard, she decided to enjoy it on the front porch. She'd just gotten herself situated on the top step when she realized she'd forgotten a fork. Leaving the plate behind, she rose to her feet and headed back inside. Her step was much lighter when she returned less than a minute later. Fork in hand, she strode to the edge of the porch. And stopped.

Her piece of pie was gone.

That couldn't be. Slices of pie didn't just disappear into thin air. *Any more than loaves of coffee cake did.* This time, the plate was missing, too.

What in the world was going on? Peering all around,

she skipped down the steps then bent over to search the ground.

"Lose something?"

Jillian jerked around. One hand flew to her mouth, the other clenched into a fist at her side. She would have screamed, but she couldn't squeeze any sound past her throat where her heart had lodged.

Twenty feet away a man materialized out of the shadows on the sidewalk.

"Luuuuuuke, it's you."

"Were you expecting an ax murderer?"

Jillian inhaled a deep breath and watched him saunter closer. He stopped just outside the circle of light spilling from the yellow bulb overhead.

"Is something wrong?" he asked.

His voice was deep. His eyes, partially hidden beneath the rim of his black hat, were colorless in the moonlight. Doing her best not to give in to the slender thread of longing that had a way of forming between them, she glanced down the street in the direction he'd just come, gauging the distance from the place she'd first noticed him to the step where she'd placed the pie.

"You didn't happen to help yourself to a slice of peach pie, did you?"

"Peach pie?"

She nodded, and he shook his head. "I'm afraid peach isn't one of my favorites. Why?"

"Oh, I was just wondering," she said, her voice falling away. "Did you see anyone else wandering around? Maybe someone carrying a slice of peach pie?"

Either he was accustomed to answering questions that didn't make any sense, or he had something else on his mind, because he shrugged one shoulder and quietly said, "Except for a couple of cats yowling on a fence over on Pike Street, I haven't seen a soul since I left the Crazy Horse. Why? What's going on?"

She was silent for a moment, thinking. "It's just that..." She shrugged, and instead of finishing what she'd been about to say, she said, "Never mind. Are you out for a late-evening stroll?"

He stepped up to the porch and hiked one boot onto the bottom step. "Actually, I've been trying to walk off a foul mood."

"Is it working?"

Luke considered her question, really he did. He hadn't been lying when he said he'd been in a foul mood, but he didn't think it would be a good idea to tell her what had brought it on. He really had gone to the Crazy Horse earlier. Unfortunately, so had Boomer Brown and Cletus McCully. Boomer had been in a jovial mood, buying rounds of drinks while going on and on about the progress he was making with the new redhead in town. Cletus had shaken his gnarly head as if it was somehow Luke's fault. Luke had stood Boomer's bragging and Cletus's censure as long as he could—which happened to be about ten minutes—then slipped out the back door without a sound.

A muscle worked in his jaw at the mere thought of the cocksure grin Boomer had been wearing. He didn't even want to think about the chastisement in Cletus's expression. Luke didn't need Cletus to tell him that someone had to try to change Jillian's mind about staying in Jasper Gulch. He'd figured that out for himself right after she'd kissed him on Main Street. *He* planned to be that someone, dammit.

That was going to be difficult enough without half the men in the county vying for her attention. Until now he'd barely had a moment alone with her, let alone time enough to convince her to give Jasper Gulch a chance. Until now he'd spent more time with horses and cattle than with her. Until now he'd...

His thoughts slowed to two words. *Until now.*

Hitching his shoulders a notch higher, he almost smiled.

He was alone with her now. Maybe he'd thank that loud-mouth Boomer for chasing him out of the Crazy Horse tonight. Nah. What Boomer didn't know wouldn't hurt him.

Feeling his confidence return, he said, "There's nothing like a brisk walk in the dark to bring a person out of a bad mood. You should give it a try."

She glanced up at him sharply. "What makes you think I'm in a bad mood?"

"Are you?"

She looked both ways down the sidewalk, then behind her into the house. "Maybe a little."

Slowly her gaze came back to his. He didn't know what was going on in her mind. Her eyes were open wide, her lips full and slightly parted. She averted her gaze as if she suddenly didn't know where to look.

"Come on, Jillian. You've made it perfectly clear where you stand with me. I'm not asking you to marry me, I'm simply asking if you'd like to accompany me on a friendly little walk."

With a slow shake of her head she said, "It wouldn't be the first one I've had today."

"The first walk?"

"The first marriage proposal."

Her soft smile caught him between the eyes, but her words sent a mental picture to his brain that grated on his nerves. "Don't tell me. Jason Tucker, right?"

This time she laughed out loud, saying, "He seemed very sincere."

"I'll bet."

Glancing behind her again, she said, "I suppose it wouldn't hurt to take a walk. I don't want to go far, though, because I wouldn't want Lisa to worry in case she comes home and finds me gone."

"We'll just go around the block."

She still didn't take that first step. "What would we talk about?"

He could think of a hundred things to talk about, a hundred questions he could ask, like what did she call that pale color of blue she was wearing, and where did she find a fabric so soft-looking and airy and thin, or what did she say to Jason Tucker's marriage request. But in the end he shrugged his shoulders and said, "Why don't you tell me how you and Lisa Markman became friends."

Luke hadn't realized he'd been holding his breath until Jillian fell into step beside him. Being careful to exhale quietly, he closed his eyes and adjusted his stride to hers.

"I first met Lisa when I was fifteen. I was living with my grandfather, and Lisa had just moved into a room in Ivy Pennington's big old house next door. I never had enough money for pretty clothes, but Lisa didn't care. She was my age, but louder, more boisterous. Although inside she was hurting more than I was. At least I had my grandfather."

Luke didn't think he'd ever grow tired of listening to the smooth cadence of Jillian's voice. When he'd first left the Crazy Horse, he'd been so agitated his boots had practically burned up the sidewalk. Now he strolled along at a snail's pace, absorbing every subtle nuance, every soft word she said.

Whether she realized it or not, he learned as much from what she didn't say as from what she said. Just as he'd suspected, she and Lisa had forged a very strong bond a long time ago. The care in her voice was too throaty to be practiced, the smile on her face too sweet to be overlooked.

"You lived with your grandfather?" he asked, turning the corner at the end of her street.

"My parents married young. Too young, my mother always said. My dad was a drifter, who came in and out of my life several times when I was very young. My mother always welcomed him back, and for a while things were good. But when I was eleven she died. By then I'd figured out that my father wasn't the sticking-around type. I knew he was sad, but somehow I also knew that when he left that time, it was going to be for good. After that I went to live with my grandfather.''

Luke listened, straining to hear at least a hint of bitterness in her voice. He knew darn well he'd have been spitting mad if his father had walked out on him. Strangely, there was no reproach in Jillian's voice or in her expression.

''Was your grandfather a good man?''

Her arm brushed his, her voice dropping even lower as she said, ''One of the best. You would have liked him. He wanted people to think he was grouchy, too.''

Luke didn't know why he suddenly felt like strutting. Yet he did. He turned his head and found Jillian staring straight ahead, awarding him a clear view of her profile. Her hair was brushed off her forehead, hanging long and wavy past her shoulders. Her nose was straight and narrow, her lips wide, her skin pale in the moonlight. He thought about skimming his fingertips along her cheekbone, but before he could raise his hand, she glanced up at him and caught him looking. His hand never made it out of his pocket. Rather than saying something she could misconstrue, he said, ''What do you mean *too?*''

Her chin came up, but whatever she saw on his features must have put her mind at ease, because she smiled and said, ''That may have sounded like an insult, but believe me, it wasn't.''

''Then you don't dislike all men.''

That caused her eyes to widen and brought out her lightning-quick response, not to mention a deep, throaty laugh. ''Now what would make you think that?''

Of their own volition, his feet stopped moving. She strolled away from him, her lightweight skirt and blouse appearing white in the moonlight. After several seconds

Luke started up again, lengthening his stride until he caught up with her. He wasn't sure his heart rate would ever catch up.

"What were you doing tonight? At the Crazy Horse, I mean," she asked.

Luke had never pretended to understand how a woman's mind functioned, but Jillian's could very well have been the most confusing of all. Doing his best to keep up with her change in topics, he said, "Wyatt and I were trying to plan the upcoming town picnic."

"Did you get very far in your plans?"

Since Luke could hardly tell her he'd come a lot closer to flattening Boomer Brown's nose, he shook his head. They turned another corner. Up ahead a yellow porch light glowed in the darkness. Their stroll around the block was coming to an end. Luke didn't want it to be over, but short of throwing her over his shoulder and stealing away into the night, he didn't see how he could prolong this time with her.

"Luke?"

"What?" he asked with a start.

"Did you?"

"Did I what?"

She looked at him strangely before saying, "Did you and Wyatt get very far in your plans?"

Her question brought him back to his senses. "So far all we've done is argue."

"Are all the men in this town so disagreeable?"

"It's this drought."

"Hmm," she said, sounding slightly distracted.

They'd reached the sidewalk leading to her front porch. Starting toward the step, he said, "The fact that most of us have been too long without a woman isn't helping matters any."

She made that humming sound again, then slowly said, "I could help."

Luke almost tripped over his own shadow. "Help?"

She turned on the bottom step. "With your picnic. I'm very organized, you know."

Pulse pounding, Luke flexed his fingers and said, "Yes, I've noticed."

"Well?" she asked, going up onto the next step. "Do you want my help?"

Her *help* wasn't all he wanted, not by a long shot, but at least a few things about Jillian Daniels were becoming clear. She had strong ties to her friends, an infectious laugh and a stubborn streak of her own. He didn't pretend to have a handle on the way her mind worked, but he couldn't deny the fact that he was intrigued.

Settling his hands on his hips, he looked up at her and said, "The whole purpose of having a town picnic is to welcome the newcomers to Jasper Gulch. It hardly seems right to expect you to help with the work."

She folded her arms in front of her and looked at the dark houses all around. "I could use something else to do. Besides, I'm not staying in Jasper Gulch, so, technically, the picnic won't be for me."

Luke could have argued, but he wasn't totally stupid. He'd been trying to find a way to spend time alone with her. It was right neighborly of her to make it so easy.

"Okay," he said quietly.

"What do you mean *okay*?"

Luke almost smiled. It was becoming a habit. "Okay, I'd appreciate any help you'd be willing to give me with planning the town picnic."

"When would you like to start?"

Feeling as if every one of his dormant wits had renewed themselves, he planted his feet a comfortable distance apart and said, "How about tomorrow night?"

Her eyes narrowed a little. "But that's a Friday night."

"What's the matter? Do you have a date?"

For a second he thought she might roll her eyes at him.

Instead she made a huffing sound that rivaled Cletus's and said, "Of course not, but you know how fast word travels in small towns, and you know how I feel about giving the wrong impression. If we spend time together, everyone will know. What will you tell the other bachelors?"

Luke narrowed his eyes, anticipation lowering his voice. "We'll tell them the truth, of course. That I saved your life, therefore your life now belongs to me." Without another word he turned and headed back the way he came.

Jillian watched him go, her heart beating a strange rhythm, his last statement echoing through her mind. His cowboy swagger was living proof that the man was too self-confident for his own good. Still she couldn't drag her gaze away. He moved in and out of the shadows with an easy grace she'd noticed before, then finally disappeared beyond the corner streetlight.

She came out of her trance slowly. Crickets were chirruping, and insects she couldn't name were answering from farther away. Luke Carson knew darn well how she felt about that little episode when he'd saved her life. Whether he admitted it or not, her life wouldn't even have been in danger, if he hadn't called to her while she was crossing the street. She didn't think for a minute that he *believed* her life now belonged to him. Yet he'd made the crack, anyway. The man really was too confident and cocky for his own good.

She went up onto the last step, thinking about how lonesome she'd been at the start of the evening. She wasn't lonesome anymore.

And she had Luke Carson to thank. Or blame.

Smiling, she walked inside.

"Tell me you don't really believe Cletus McCully is sweet."

The tip of Jillian's pencil snapped. "Luke, I'm trying to plan a picnic here."

"You're the one who brought it up."

"I was thinking out loud."

"That always gets me in trouble."

Although he shifted in his chair like a rambunctious child who'd had all he could take of sitting still, there was nothing childish about his expression or about the way his shoulders filled out his faded cotton shirt. The sleeves were rolled up on his forearms, the buttons open at his throat. He had a strong neck and a face that was shaped by clear-cut lines and shallow hollows. The squint lines next to his eyes were befitting a man in his mid-thirties, but the playful glint in their depths made him appear younger than his actual years.

"You know what they say about all work and no play, Jillian."

She shook her head. No wonder the members of the town council hadn't gotten very far in their plans. Reaching for another pencil, she said, "I never said I wasn't dull. Now come on, we're almost finished."

Without conscious thought, Luke covered her hand with his, watching as her gaze followed the movement, then slowly came back to his face. Her eyes were wide open, her lips full and slightly parted. He'd meant his touch to be a prelude to a much-needed break, little more than a token of friendliness. Friendly, hell. The merest brush of his fingers against her skin sent need up his arm, straight to his gut.

He didn't understand it. He'd known this woman for less than a week. Strangely, his body didn't care. An explosion went through him every time he came within ten feet of her, pulling at his senses, obliterating his thoughts. He knew these feelings were too new to be acted upon. But they were too real to be ignored.

She pulled her hand away and averted her gaze as if she was uneasy with the relationship that was developing between them. He didn't want her to be uncomfortable, and he certainly didn't want her to hide her feelings from him. Hoping to put them back on an even footing, he reached across his kitchen table and held up several sheets of paper.

"I'd hardly call you dull, Jillian. But just look at all the work we've already accomplished tonight. You've arranged for the Anderson brothers to play their country music. Here's a list of everything Wyatt, Clayt and I need to talk to Isabell Pruitt and the members of the Ladies Aid Society about. You've designed flyers, and you've even made a note about contacting someone about supplying portable bathrooms. I knew you were organized, but I didn't know you were a slave driver. Honestly, you're starting to remind me of my seventh-grade history teacher."

Jillian looked up, straight into Luke's gray eyes. He was teasing her. She could tell by the way those eyes of his smiled a full five seconds before his mouth did. Even so, when his lips moved to reveal the even edge of his teeth, she wasn't prepared for her body's reaction, wasn't prepared for the subtle softening of her heart or the swelling, swaying sensation in her chest.

"I think that was the highest compliment I've ever received," she said quietly.

He stared at her for a long moment. And then, with the lift of one eyebrow, he said, "You obviously haven't met Edith Ferguson."

Jillian laughed out loud. The man's cocksure attitude and subtle wit never ceased to amaze her. She'd noticed his restless energy before, but it had never been more apparent than tonight. He wasn't a man who enjoyed sitting still.

Pushing the papers littering the tabletop into a pile, she said, "I'll have to look her up. Maybe she wouldn't mind sharing a few teaching tips with me."

"You're a teacher?"

Bringing her index finger down to her thumb, she said,

"I'm this close to obtaining my very first teaching position."

Luke pushed away from the table and walked to the other side of the room, where he leaned against the counter. He waited to ask the question that was screaming inside his head until after he'd crossed his ankles and his arms. In a tone of voice that was as casual as he could manage, he said, "A teaching position in Madison?"

She smiled. Actually it was more like a grin from ear to ear. He didn't think he'd ever seen that particular brand of excitement on her face, or heard so much quiet happiness in her voice as she said, "I know I'm a little older than the average college graduate. After all, most people don't cram a four-year degree into ten years like I did. Still, the principal at the elementary school there seemed very impressed with my résumé. I've gotten through two interviews, and according to other teachers in the area, if I'm called in for a third, the job is mine."

Luke didn't like the sound of this. He'd invited her out here tonight to get to know her better. In the process he'd learned that she had a very good reason for insisting that she wasn't planning to stay in Jasper Gulch. There must have been a story behind her quip about her four-year degree taking ten years. Now he wasn't so sure he wanted to hear it. He already knew she'd had some tough breaks in her life. But those had been a long time ago and really would have no effect on whether or not she stayed in South Dakota.

A teaching position she'd struggled years to obtain was another matter.

"You're probably right," she said, placing the papers in a folder. "We've covered enough for one night."

That sounded like the beginning of goodbye. It was all Luke could do to keep from swearing out loud.

He didn't want her to leave. *Then you'd better think fast, Carson, or she's going to do just that.*

"I guess I'll see you on Monday."

Taking his time uncrossing his ankles, he said, "It's not that late, Jillian."

"But you said we've covered enough of the details for the upcoming picnic."

"Are you in a hurry to get home?"

"No." She turned around slowly, stretching the word out to about ten letters.

"Good. So tell me, is this your first *visit* to South Dakota?"

This time she was the one shaking her head as if she couldn't quite follow the change in topics. Luke preferred it this way.

"Then you haven't seen the stars from out here. Come on, I know a place with the perfect view."

With a skeptical lift of her eyebrows, she asked, "And where might that be?"

The light over the table shot several strands of her red hair with a golden glow and intensified the misgivings in her eyes. Taking one step closer, he said, "Suspicious, aren't you? For your information, I wasn't thinking about looking at the sky from the bed of my truck. I was going to suggest the fence out back."

He gave her a few seconds to mull it over, then turned and strode through his back door. He hoped he looked more sure of himself than he felt. While he was at it, he hoped she didn't hear him heave a relieved sigh at the first sound of her footsteps behind him.

He shortened his stride, and together they sauntered toward the fenced-in area in the distance, where he occasionally kept horses or cattle for observation and safekeeping. The fence was made of rough-hewn logs, some straight, some not. It wasn't painted, and it sure wasn't fancy, but it served its purpose well. Luke remembered the weekend he, Clayt and Wyatt had dug the holes and set the posts, when he'd first bought this place the year after he'd started his vet service. He'd climbed onto this fence at least a thousand times in the past ten years, but until tonight he'd never invited a woman to sit on it with him.

He swung onto the top log while Jillian settled on a slightly bowed section a few feet away. Light flickered across the sky far in the distance. Like a hundred spotlights, it wavered off and on and off again.

"That's heat lightning," he said. "It's been teasing us for weeks. We sure could use the real thing around here."

Raising her face to the sky, she said, "It may be teasing you, but it sure is beautiful. Remind me not to question your authority when it comes to views. That sky is spectacular."

Luke didn't think there had been anything lust arousing about her exclamation. And there was certainly nothing erotic about her faded cutoffs or pale yellow T-shirt, or about the way her hair was pulled away from her face and secured with a yellow ribbon partway down her back. Yet there was a certain femininity in her hairstyle and an enticing hint of temptation in the length of thigh not covered by her shorts.

He would have liked to challenge her to try to match this view in Madison, but he was afraid she'd tell him she knew of a place there where the view was even better. For the first time in his life he didn't know what to say. Why wouldn't he be tongue-tied? This was the first time he'd known a woman who wasn't impressed by the width of his shoulders or the tilt of his black Stetson. The strange thing was that for the first time in his life he wanted a woman to see beyond either of those things.

It was a sobering realization, but the heat pulsing through him certainly wasn't. Ironically, he felt more alive than he had in years, while the rest of the countryside was burning up a little more every day.

"What are you thinking about?"

Her voice was soft, her face still tipped toward the sky.

He felt an almost overwhelming wish that she'd turn toward him and slowly lean closer. He couldn't remember the last time he'd felt this way. The beating rhythm of his heart told him it had little to do with the fact that there had been a noted lack of women in the area and everything to do with the fact that *this* woman was here with him now.

"Luke?"

He turned toward her with a start. She'd asked him what he was thinking. Scrambling to come up with an answer, he said, "Oh, this and that. And the drought."

"Tell me about your drought."

He stared at her profile in disbelief. He was finally alone with a her in the dark, and she wanted to talk about the weather. He could think of several topics he'd rather discuss, each and every one of them having to do with hot, sultry nights and long, slow kisses. And she wanted to talk about the drought.

Sighing in resignation, he said, "It started out as speculation by some of the old-timers who had nothing better to do than sit around and spread their gloom and doom. We had a mild winter with a less than average snowfall. Nothing to be too concerned about. But then the spring showers were few and far between. Now we haven't seen so much as a sprinkle in well over a month. As bad as this is, it's nothing compared to the drought that gripped the area in the thirties. That one lasted ten years. The way some of the old-timers tell it, the dust storms were so thick they called them black blizzards. I hope to high heaven things don't come to that now."

"What will the ranchers do if the drought continues?" she asked.

"Other than worry and complain, there's not much they can do. The creeks and rivers aren't completely dry yet. But if it doesn't rain soon, the animals will get rangy, unpredictable and eventually, sick. If the drought goes on for more than another week or two, I'm going to contact agencies farther east and get the ball rolling to have water trucked in and carried to the livestock and horses.''

"Cletus McCully told me you'd probably do that.''

Luke glanced at her speculatively. "Just how often do you talk to Cletus McCully?''

"Every morning on my way to the post office, why?''

He made a derogatory sound deep in his throat. "Don't get me started.''

"I don't know how you can dislike him. Why, he reminds me a little of you.''

Luke almost fell off the fence. His reaction seemed to amuse her, which only made him clench his teeth tighter. "If you're trying to make me humble, it's working. First you insinuate that I'm grouchy, too, and now you're telling me I remind you of a seventy-nine-year-old man.''

"A man who's as sweet as day.''

He waited a moment to answer, letting her words soak into his senses, savoring the feeling of satisfaction they left in the deep recesses of his mind. "Is that how you see me, Jillian?'' he asked, his voice a husky rasp in the quiet night. "As sweet as day?''

Jillian turned her head slowly and found Luke looking at her. She had half a mind to tell him that there was nothing sweet about him, but she caught a glimpse of something in his eyes, something deeper than irreverence, more subtle than his masculine conceit. She had a difficult time forming an answer, because the other things she saw weren't going to be easy to forget. There was goodness and steadfastness, honesty, and yes, if she looked deep enough, she saw sweetness, too.

Closing her eyes, she reminded herself that she couldn't allow herself to be distracted by romantic notions. In an instant she thought of everything she'd worked for these past twelve years, everything she'd dreamed of, everything she'd hoped for. Jillian Daniels, the poor girl from Wisconsin, the girl who had to work ten times harder to get where she was today, was almost there.

There wasn't in Jasper Gulch.

Okay, maybe she was here now. But not for long. And certainly not forever.

She used the time it took to climb down from the fence to get her thoughts in order. Once her feet were firmly on the ground, she reached her hand toward Luke. Placing her palm on his cheek, she said, "Trust me. It's better for both of us if I don't answer that question."

With that she turned and strode to her friend's car, which was parked in the driveway near the house. Luke was left sitting on his own fence on the outskirts of town, his mouth hanging open, his mind reeling from her touch.

Gradually his thoughts cleared. He closed his mouth and stared at the headlights of the car that was slowly backing from his driveway. Jillian might have believed that she hadn't answered him, but she was wrong. Her answer had been in the gentle touch of her fingertips and in the sultry tone of her voice. She cared about him. For some reason she was fighting it with everything she had.

Sliding off the fence to the ground, he wondered what it would take to finally get her to admit it to herself. He hoped he could figure out a way to make it happen *before* she was offered that teaching position and left Jasper Gulch for good.

Chapter Five

"Let's see," Jillian said, peering from the kitchen into the living room, where the front porch was partially visible through the screen door. "The card table and chairs are set up. I even pressed your linen tablecloth. The dishes are slightly mismatched, but the balloons on the backs of the chairs are bobbing in the breeze, and if you ask me, it looks like the perfect celebration supper."

Lisa peeked into the oven. "Ivy's fidget pie is already cooling outside. All I'm waiting for are the rolls."

Satisfied that there was nothing more she could do except wait, Jillian leaned against the counter and asked, "How in the world did Ivy sneak that frozen meat-and-potato pie in without our knowledge?"

"I think she had Cori and Allison divert our attention until she'd packed it in the bottom of the cooler," Lisa said, reaching into the refrigerator for the pitcher of lemonade.

She poured the beverage into two glasses then handed one to Jillian. Jillian took a long sip, the ice-cold liquid cooling a trail from her lips all the way down to the pit of her stomach, making her feel the tiniest bit giddy. Today marked the one-week anniversary of her and Lisa's arrival into town, and tonight was the eve before the grand opening of the Jasper Gulch Clothing Store.

After taking another long sip of her lemonade, she placed the glass on the counter behind her. "You haven't told me how your latest date went last night, Lisa."

Lisa dropped her shoulders and blew a wisp of hair out of her eyes. "That's because there isn't much to tell."

"Then Grover Andrews isn't the man for you, either?"

Lisa shook her head. "Can you really picture me with a man named Grover?"

Jillian smiled at the expression on her friend's face. "You can't judge a man by his name. Grover Cleveland was a good man, wasn't he?"

"Yes, but did Grover Cleveland chew a wad of tobacco the size of a golf ball and live with his mother when he was forty-three?"

Jillian laughed at Lisa's irreverent tone. "For a person who's intent upon finding a man, you're being awfully picky."

"I hardly think I'm being picky just because I happen to believe that somewhere out there is a man who would be perfect for me. A man a little beaten up by life. Maybe a cowboy or an ex-rodeo rider. A man who's gruff on the outside and sweet on the inside."

Jillian stared at a bead of condensation slowly zigzagging down the side of her glass, her thoughts following a similar pattern. Lisa's description of the kind of man she was searching for called to mind one tall, rugged, *sweet* man Jillian had been trying *not* to think about all weekend. She told herself it shouldn't have been so difficult. She'd put men out of her mind before. Apparently her memories of Luke were as stubborn as he was.

That's all it was, she told herself. Stubbornness. It had nothing to do with this gentle softening inside her chest, or with a strange, deep-seated yearning she hadn't felt in years. Even if it did have to do with either of those things, she wasn't really worried. After all, forewarned was forearmed. She had her life planned, her future mapped out. She was going to be the kind of teacher that would have made her grandfather proud. While she was at it, she was going to make herself proud, striving to see the potential in even the shyest child, the way her tenth-grade English teacher had done with her.

Staying in Jasper Gulch simply wasn't in her plans. Neither was falling in love. *That* particular emotion may have been written in Lisa's stars, but not in hers. Oh, no. Jillian didn't plan to fall in love ever again.

The thought came unbidden. On its heels came another. It would probably be a good idea if she didn't allow herself to get attached to Luke Carson. She'd continue to work for him, but that was all. No more late-night walks, and no more stargazing on fences just outside of town. From now on, she was going to keep it strictly professional.

That decision made, she reached for her glass and said, "Maybe you'll meet someone at the town picnic this weekend."

Leaning down to check on the rolls again, Lisa said, "Maybe. That reminds me. Cletus tells me I have you to thank for the marvelous coincidence that the store's grand opening just happens to fall during the week prior to the town's biggest event in years. Cletus says that every town deserving a name needs a Western clothing store, and I say he's right. Everyone who goes to the picnic will be wanting new clothes. The store is going to be a success, I just know it."

Jillian smiled and said, "With you running it, how could it be anything else?"

Smiling back, Lisa closed the oven door with one hip and said, "If you get the salad, I'll take the rolls. Ivy's fidget pie should be the perfect temperature to eat. Come on, Jillian, our celebration supper is being served.''

Jillian took the bowl of freshly tossed salad from the refrigerator, reached for her glass of lemonade, then hurried after Lisa. ''Well,'' she said before the screen door had banged shut behind her. ''What do you think?''

''I'll be doggoned.''

Jillian strode onto the porch where she peered at her friend's face. Lisa was staring at the table, her mouth and eyes wide with surprise and disbelief. Jillian glanced down, her smile freezing on her face.

Ivy's pie was gone.

She looked at the hedge closest to the porch, then across the street and finally at the house on the other side of the driveway. Two boys wearing cowboy hats rode past on their bikes, a little girl trailing behind on her tricycle. A neighbor's television droned from another house farther away. The scene looked as innocent as any Norman Rockwell painting ever had.

''Maybe Cletus McCully was wrong,'' Lisa said. ''Maybe the color of orange that Bonnie Trumble painted her beauty parlor isn't Jasper Gulch's biggest crime after all.''

Jillian's stomach rumbled. She hadn't been too upset about the missing coffee cake or the slice of peach pie. As far as she knew, the cake really could have been taken by a stray dog, and she'd assumed the missing piece of pie was the result of a prank by a local teenager. But both the cake and the piece of pie had been taken in the dark of night. Now it was only seven o'clock, which meant that Ivy's fidget pie had disappeared in broad daylight.

''That's strange.''

Lisa's voice brought Jillian from her musings. ''What's strange?''

''Whoever took Ivy's pie took our balloons, too.''

Jillian did a double take. Sure enough, the balloons

she'd tied to the backs of their chairs were gone. She didn't really care about the balloons, and she could find something else to eat for supper, but whoever had taken Ivy's pie had taken her casserole dish, too. That dish was old, and a gift from their dear, gray-haired friend back home.

"Lisa, there's a pie thief in this town."

"Yes, it certainly looks that way."

Placing her glass of lemonade on the table, Jillian went perfectly still.

"Jillian, you're getting that look."

"What look is that?"

"The one you get when you're about to get involved in a worthy cause."

Jillian didn't bother trying to disguise her rising indignation. "This was no fluke, Lisa. Someone is purposefully stealing from our front porch. And something has to be done."

"Well I'll be a monkey's uncle."

Cletus McCully drew his bushy gray eyebrows together and released an airy whistle. "Somebody swiped your supper right off your porch?"

At Jillian's nod the old man pushed himself to his feet in front of his favorite bench and assumed the stance she'd come to recognize, his legs slightly bowed, his shoulders slightly stooped, his thumbs hooked through his suspenders.

"Do you have any idea who might have done such a thing?" she asked.

Cletus snapped one suspender and rubbed his craggy chin. "Nope, nope, can't say that I do. One thing folks in these parts have is plenty of food. They're more likely to give it away than take it. Why, it's a standing joke out here that the only time a body has to lock his doors is during zucchini season. Not this year, of course, on account of the drought. But I still can't imagine anybody stealing food. Why, just the other day I was tellin' Ed down at the barbershop..."

While Cletus rambled on, Jillian cast an unhurried glance up the street. Mertyl Gentry was sweeping the sidewalk in front of the grocery store just like she did every morning at eight-thirty sharp. There wasn't any activity in front of the Crazy Horse, but Jillian could hear the hydraulic hoist going up in Hal Everts garage two doors down. A few people sauntered into Mel's Diner for breakfast, but the undisputed busiest place on the block was the Jasper Gulch Clothing Store. Bachelors of every size and shape milled in, only to come out again a short time later wearing a grin and carrying their purchases in one of Lisa's new Jasper Gulch Clothing Store logo-emblazoned bags.

Keeping her voice low enough to be discreet but loud enough to be heard over the noise of an old pickup truck rattling by, Jillian said, "It all seemed spookier last night, but now, well, I think I'm just going to let it pass."

Cletus let loose a harrumph that was bigger than he was and straightened to his full height, stoop-shouldered though it might be. "We can't let folks steal food right off your table. Something has to be done."

"I thought the same thing when I locked the doors last night, Cletus, but it isn't easy to stay unnerved about a little stolen food when everything appears so peaceful and normal now that the sun is up. After all, what's really been taken? Two balloons, a little food and an old casserole dish that has a high sentimental value but isn't really worth more than three dollars and fifty cents."

"Stealin' is stealin'."

"Do you really think so?" she asked.

"I know so. Now you've gotta march next door to my grandson's office and tell him what you just told me."

Taking a step backward, she asked, "You want me to tell the sheriff?"

"It's your civic duty."

"But I'm on my way to the post office for Luke's..."

"Petty thievery could very well lead to bigger things. Jumping catfish, we can't have that here in Jasper Gulch."

"I know, Cletus, but..."

"Now listen up, young lady. Here's whatcha gotta do."

Jillian didn't know what to make of the strangely knowing look on Cletus's lined face, but try as she might, she couldn't get a word in edgewise. Since she couldn't very well offend the man, she folded her arms and listened to what he had to say. Five minutes later he was lowering his bony frame onto the wooden bench, and she was heading for the sheriff's office twenty-five feet away.

Cletus muttered something she couldn't make out, but when she glanced over her shoulder, he gave her a toothy grin and a hearty nod before gesturing for her to keep going. She reached for the doorknob, hoping the old sweetheart wasn't becoming delusionary from spending so much time on that bench in the sweltering heat.

Before she could finish the thought, the doorknob turned beneath her hand. The next thing she knew, she was face-to-face with Luke Carson and Sheriff Wyatt McCully.

"Jillian, what are you doing here?"

"Can I help you?"

The men had spoken at the same time, making it difficult to know who to answer first. She cast a surreptitious look at Cletus, who was nodding in earnest now. Sighing away her hesitation, she turned to the man in uniform and said, "Cletus suggested I come in and talk to you, Sheriff, but since you're on your way out, I'll come back another time."

"No, no. Luke and I were just putting the finishing touches on the plans you helped him make for the town picnic. Come in, come in," the sheriff said, ushering her inside.

Jillian followed them, taking in the furnishings with one

sweeping glance. The office could have come straight from the set of the old Andy Griffith shows Ivy had watched back in Madison, from the old desk and filing cabinets to the railing dividing the room. However, the resemblance didn't carry over to the two men waiting for her to speak. Wyatt McCully was nearly as tall as Luke, his shoulders nearly as broad. His hair was blond, his eyes the same shade of brown as his grandfather's, and although he looked strong enough to handle most situations, he appeared to be the type of lawman who spent more time rescuing kittens out of trees than arresting hardened criminals. It was a comforting thought and made the very idea that there could be a real criminal in Jasper Gulch seem even more ludicrous.

From the other side of the old metal desk, Wyatt said, "What seems to be the trouble?"

"I don't...I mean, I'm not..." Pulling herself together, she finally said, "I'm afraid coming here was a mistake."

"My grandfather wouldn't have sent you if he didn't believe it was serious."

Wyatt sank into his chair and steepled his fingers, causing Jillian to wonder if her first impression of him might have been wrong. Maybe he was more adept at catching criminals than she'd thought.

"Please," he said, pointing to a vacant chair, "have a seat."

Luke waited to see what Jillian would do, not entirely certain she'd take the chair Wyatt had offered. She fiddled with the clasp on her purse, distributing her weight from one foot to the other. For lack of anything better to do, he strode to a small table on the far wall and poured coffee into three mugs.

He'd shown up at Wyatt's office an hour ago and needed more caffeine like he needed a hole in his head. But at least pouring coffee gave him something to do and a reason to stay.

He'd told Wyatt about the teaching position Jillian was planning to take more than five hundred miles away. The two men had been friends for thirty years, but Wyatt didn't have much to offer in the way of advice where changing one red-haired school teacher's mind was concerned. Consequently, Luke was no closer to finding a solution than he'd been Friday night.

When he'd first hired Jillian, he thought he'd have countless opportunities to be alone with her. Alone, hell. Yesterday eleven bachelors had shown up at the office with a *sick* pet. And he didn't even have clinic hours on Mondays. Most of them brought dogs, but a few carted in their mothers' house cats. A bachelor from a neighboring town had dragged in a barn cat who'd never seen the inside of a house, let alone the inside of a veterinarian's office. That old tomcat had been spitting mad. By the end of the morning so had Luke.

But whether the boys knew it or not, their ploy hadn't worked. According to reliable sources Jillian hadn't accepted a date from a single one of them. Oh, no. She was too smart for that.

Luke wasn't sorry she was smart. In fact, her intelligence and quick wit were half of what made her so appealing. He'd spent a good part of the previous night trying not to think about some of her other appealing attributes, trying not to imagine the scent of her shampoo or the gentle sway of her hips and how soft the skin at the base of her throat looked and how heavy her breasts would feel in the palm of his hands. He'd awakened to the whir of a fan, warm and wanting in both mind and body, his pillows on the floor, the sheets a tangled heap at his feet.

That telltale heat was pooling low in his belly right now. Scrubbing a hand over his face, he picked up the mugs of coffee and strode back to Wyatt's desk where Jillian was talking, perched on the edge of her chair.

"Last night my friend and I were preparing to sit down to dinner..."

"Your friend with the dark brown hair?" Wyatt asked.

If Wyatt noticed Luke's irreverent little snort or the coffee sloshing over the side of the mug being pushed his way, he didn't let on. Not that Luke was surprised. Wyatt McCully could keep his thoughts to himself better than anyone he'd ever known. It was one of the things that made him such a good lawman, not to mention the best poker player in the county.

With a small nod Jillian said, "Last night Lisa and I set up the card table on the porch where it was cooler. When we walked outside to eat, we discovered that our main course was gone."

"Gone?" Wyatt asked.

"Stolen," Jillian explained.

"Are you saying that someone right here in Jasper Gulch stole your supper?"

She nodded, then shrugged. "Actually, this time they only took the balloons and the main course."

"This time?" Wyatt asked.

Luke jerked forward in his chair. He managed to remain silent, but if *he* had asked the question, it would have been in a voice that was a helluva lot louder than Wyatt's.

What did she mean *this time?*

"This has happened before?" Wyatt prodded.

"Well," she said, sliding back in her chair. "The first time, Lisa and I assumed a stray dog must have been responsible. But then, a few nights ago, a slice of peach pie disappeared. You remember, Luke. That was the night you happened to be walking by."

Wyatt's gaze swung to Luke as if he was following a bouncing ball. Holding up both hands, Luke said, "She said it was *peach* pie."

Wyatt accepted his explanation without a word. Why wouldn't he? Luke really *didn't* like peach pie. Even if he did, he wouldn't stoop so low as to swipe it from Jillian's front porch.

"What time were these items taken?" Wyatt asked.

"That's what's so weird. The pie and coffee cake disappeared late at night, but whoever took Ivy's fidget pie did it in broad daylight."

"Fidget pie?" Wyatt asked.

"It's an old-fashioned English pot pie made with meat and potatoes and apples."

Nodding, Wyatt pulled open a drawer and asked, "Did you see or hear anything?"

Jillian shook her head. "Not a sound. There were no footprints, either. And nothing was spilled that might leave a trail."

Luke placed his coffee cup on the desk and looked at Jillian, his thoughts coming in quick succession. He'd been wondering how he was going to change her mind about staying when she seemed so adamant about leaving. He wasn't going to be able to convince her during office hours, that was for sure. And now that the picnic was all planned, he hadn't had the foggiest idea how he was going to get close to her after dark, when she'd made her stand perfectly clear. He'd been wracking his brain trying to come up with some other way. It was mighty nice of her to hand him the opportunity on a silver platter, or should he say on her friend's casserole dish? Steepling his fingers the way Wyatt often did, he bided his time, waiting for the perfect moment to set his plan into motion.

"My grandfather was right to send you here," Wyatt declared, sliding a sheet of paper across the desk. "Now, if you'll just sign at the bottom, the complaint will be formal."

"You want me to sign a formal complaint?"

"As soon as you do, I'll start investigating. When I have enough evidence, I'll make the arrest."

Jillian jumped to her feet so fast her white jeans and

pale pink shirt blurred before Luke's eyes. "Sheriff, I didn't come here to get anyone in trouble."

"*You're* not getting anyone in trouble. Whoever is taking your food is doing that on his own," Wyatt said, also rising to his feet.

Watching the interaction from his chair, Luke wanted to applaud Wyatt's reasoning. Jillian didn't appear to share Wyatt's aplomb. She turned in a half circle, shaking her head. "I don't want to file a formal complaint. I just want the incidents to stop. And if possible I'd like this person to return Ivy's dish."

Luke supposed he shouldn't have been surprised that Jillian didn't want to harm anyone, but he felt a little awestruck just the same. She'd obviously lived through some tough times, yet she hadn't become hard or cynical or bitter. A woman like her was a rarity. No wonder he wanted her so badly.

His adrenaline kicked in as if someone had thrown a switch, steadily making its way from one end of his body to the other. Striving for a steady tone of voice, he said, "We're going to need some bait."

Two heads pivoted in his direction.

"Bait?" Wyatt asked.

"We?" Jillian said at the same time.

Instead of answering immediately, Luke took his time unsteepling his fingers and reaching to the desk for his hat, loving the powerful emotions pulsing through him. *Luke Carson, you are good.*

He slapped his hat against his thigh one time and rose to his feet. "This is probably as innocent as one of the bachelors vying for attention. Jillian's right, Wyatt. There's no need to involve the law." Turning to Jillian, he said, "We'll need some kind of food to use as bait. If you don't mind, I'll let you rustle that up. Now I have some cattle to inoculate at Jed Harely's place west of town.

I'll see you tonight just after dark.''

He shoved his hat on his head and, with a devil of a smile, sauntered out the front door.

Other than the light spilling from the kitchen, the living room was dark. And far too quiet, despite the twangy voice wafting to Jillian's ears from the radio in the corner. Pressing her shoulders against the wall underneath the open window, she wet her lower lip and stole a glance at the man sitting next to her.

As usual, Luke's blue cotton shirt looked clean and well worn, the lines of his masculine profile well defined. He smelled of soap and summer. His medium brown hair, slightly shaggy around the edges, looked almost black in the darkness. His legs were drawn up, his forearms resting on his knees. She'd never seen him so relaxed, while she'd never felt so fidgety.

She'd been this way ever since he'd sauntered out of the sheriff's office that morning, leaving her and Wyatt standing there with their mouths gaping open and their coffee getting cold. She'd come out of her stupor enough to mumble a hurried goodbye to the sheriff before heading next door to get the mail. But she still hadn't recovered her equilibrium. This was totally unlike her.

She'd tried to throttle the dizzying current racing through her bloodstream, but to no avail. Even nearly running off her feet all afternoon in Lisa's store hadn't chased her unease away.

Luke, on the other hand, appeared completely at ease. True to his word, he'd arrived shortly after dark, sauntering into the kitchen with that loose-jointed swagger nearly every cowboy out here possessed. He might have been a tad bit more lofty than the other men she'd met, but she supposed that went with the territory. After all, he was the only veterinarian in an area whose people depended upon their animals for their livelihood. None of those things explained the reason for her own jitters. And they certainly didn't explain why her gaze kept straying to his mouth. She swallowed hard, her thoughts fragmenting.

Searching for something to say that might ease the tension inside her, she whispered, "Do you think Lisa's lasagna is still out there?"

He shrugged one shoulder, his shirt collar grazing the wall as he whispered, "Did you hear something?"

Jillian shook her head. "I haven't heard anything except country-western music since we sat down here on the floor twenty minutes ago."

He straightened his legs and crossed his ankles, his boots creaking slightly as he said, "My mother always says there are two kinds of music out here. New country-western music, and *old* country-western music."

Jillian didn't think she'd ever heard a man whisper in tones so low and mellow. She'd met Luke's father and brother, but until now he'd never mentioned his mother. *Her* mother had died three days before Jillian's twelfth birthday. She'd had her grandfather, and now she had wonderful friends, but there was something about families that fascinated her.

Thankful to have at last found a safe topic, she said, "What's your mother like?"

"There's a question."

There was a hint of exasperation in his voice, but if Jillian wasn't mistaken, he was smiling when he continued. "She's five feet two inches of pure feminine wile. She's tenderhearted, but she's strong, too. She'd have to be to put up with my father for thirty-eight years."

"Then they're still together?" Jillian asked quietly.

"Oh, they're together, all right. Although when she called a few nights ago my father threatened to move all her things out to the barn if she doesn't get her fanny back home where she belongs."

Jillian was so intrigued she forgot about her earlier tension. "Do you mean she isn't here in Jasper Gulch?"

"She went back to Oregon almost a month ago to help her sisters take care of my ailing grandmother. My mother will be back, but not before she's good and ready. I wouldn't be surprised if she stayed in Oregon for another month, at least."

Staring at the oblong patch of light stretching through the kitchen doorway, Jillian felt herself smile. "The rest of her family lives in Oregon?"

She sensed Luke's nod more than saw it, just as she sensed that he was about to say more. "They met when my father did a stint in the Navy. The way he tells it, she took one look at him and knew he was the man for her. Dad claims she was on him like a blanket on a horse. Personally, I think it was the other way around. Anyway, he married her and brought her back here. I don't imagine there's another woman who could have held her own with the Carson men."

"Don't tell me you and Clayt gave her a hard time while you were growing up."

The exaggerated shake of his head said a lot more than words could have.

"What did you two do?" she whispered.

Luke didn't say anything for a long moment. He was sitting in a darkened room with a beautiful woman, and the last thing he wanted to do was talk about his family. Hell, he didn't want to talk. Period. Jillian was so close he could hear her breathing, could smell the flowery scent of her shampoo. He would have liked to move closer, but she'd been as jumpy as a cat on hot bricks since he'd stepped inside the house.

She was calmer now, and since he didn't want her to send him on his way, he decided to answer her question. "You may find this hard to believe, but I wasn't always so agreeable and easygoing."

She made a disparaging sound deep in her throat and waited for him to continue.

"Clayt is twelve months and six days older than me. According to our father, we started fighting the day they brought me home from the hospital."

"I thought you were best friends."

"We are, but as kids we were too much alike to get along. The older we got, the worse our fights became. One day when I was twelve, we were pounding each other good when our mother walked in. We were both taller than she was by then, but it made no difference to her. She grabbed us by the shirt collars and hauled us, still swinging, to our feet. The next thing we knew she let out a yelp and her hand flew to her mouth. All three of us froze as her lip swelled to twice its normal size."

On a whisper Jillian asked, "One of you hit her?"

"Not on purpose. Clayt and I have never known which one, but yes, we were responsible."

"What did she do?"

"She left the room without saying a word. Clayt and I sank to the couch, feeling sicker than the night we snuck a bottle of Dad's best whiskey up to our room. We were in big trouble. And we both knew it. Dad's bark had always been worse than his bite, but we knew that *that* called for the strap if anything did."

Luke hadn't thought about that day in years, yet it came back to him as if it had happened last week. He would never forget how horrible he'd felt. Good God, for once he and Clayt hadn't hurt each other. They'd bruised their *mother.* To this day he remembered how he'd felt sitting on that sofa, hoping for an early and painless death.

"Did your father use the strap on you?"

"He didn't get the chance. Mom came back, planted her size-six feet in front of us and said, 'Boys, I want to make a deal. I'm not going to tell your father about this. After all, you're the only children I have. But I want your word that neither of you will ever raise a fist to the other again.'

"At the time we would have promised her anything.

When Clayt reminded her that Dad would notice the bruise, she said, 'I'm going to tell your father I got kicked checking Prancer's shoe.'"

Jillian asked, "She lied on your behalf?"

Luke shook his head. "We asked her the same thing, but she told us she was going to go out to the barn and bother Prancer until he did just that. First she wanted our word."

Luke was quiet for a minute, remembering. He'd been tall for a twelve-year-old and hadn't cried in years. But tears had rolled down his face that day as he'd said, "We give you our word, but tell Dad. We'll take the whipping."

Rita Carson had raised her chin, turned on her heel and walked out to the barn.

"She never told your father?" Jillian asked quietly.

Luke shrugged. "To this day I don't know. It doesn't matter. Clayt and I haven't raised our fists to each other since. After all, a Carson is only as good as his word."

Jillian barely moved, not even to breathe. In the background, Reba was singing about the greatest man she never knew. The words seemed fitting somehow. It was strange, but until that moment Jillian had always thought people's lives could only be changed by tragedy. Luke's life had been shaped by something just as powerful. He'd said a Carson was only as good as his word. Whether he knew it or not, he was very good, indeed.

Earlier, tension had filled her chest. Sometime during Luke's whispered reminiscing, the tension had drained out of her, only to be replaced by a gentle swelling, swaying sensation around her heart.

She turned her head and found Luke looking at her in the darkness. Her eyelashes fluttered down then back up again; everything inside her going perfectly still. He touched her face, his fingers splaying wide through her hair, his palm heating her like sunshine. It had been a long time since she'd felt warm in exactly this way. It had been a long time since she'd missed it.

Before he'd arrived, she'd gone over and over what she would say and how she would act. She'd vowed to stay focused on the reason he was here tonight and on the reason she wouldn't stay here forever. Now she knew only two things. He was going to kiss her. And she was going to let him.

She placed her palm flat on the floor for leverage and slowly raised her chin. He leaned closer, and so did she, his breath warming her cheek, his features blurring before her eyes.

She felt a tiny vibration beneath her hand, and somewhere in the deep recesses of her mind she was aware of a sound on the other side of the window, a soft thud of footsteps on the porch.

Her heart pounded and her thoughts slowed. She raised her face another inch, and he lowered his just as far. His lips touched hers in a kiss as light and tender as a summer breeze. But then their lips parted, and the kiss changed, deepening, at once urgent and exploratory, mysterious yet familiar. Pleasure radiated outward from the joining of their lips, broadening like ripples on a lake, making her sigh.

His heart beat a steady rhythm beneath her left hand. As his mouth moved closer for another kiss, she felt another kind of vibration beneath her other hand as more footsteps thudded on the porch.

The porch.

Her eyes opened. And so did his. For the span of one heartbeat they both froze.

"Footsteps," he whispered.

"On the porch," she gasped.

"The pie thief!" they said at the same time.

Chapter Six

Luke and Jillian stumbled to their feet. Her knee nudged his thigh; his shoulder clipped her chin. With a series of thuds and thumps, they felt their way around an overstuffed chair and ottoman then burst through the screen door.

"Damn."

Squinting against the sudden brightness of the porch light, Jillian could only stare at the empty table. The thief had struck again. She strode to the porch railing while Luke hurried to the sidewalk out front where he peered into the shadows in every direction. She could tell by the way he raked one hand through his hair that whoever had taken the lasagna was long gone.

Glancing behind her, she shook her head. Some detective she'd turned out to be. She'd been sitting underneath the open window on the other side of that very wall. She'd heard footsteps, but she'd been too preoccupied to react. All because Luke had kissed her.

Or had she kissed him?

The question was dredged from a place beyond logic or

reason, from a place where there were only shadowy feelings and shimmering emotions, dusky yearnings and hidden dreams. In retrospect she knew he *had* kissed her, just as she knew she'd kissed him in return. All because she'd wanted to.

She closed her eyes, banishing the thought. When she opened them again, Luke was walking toward her, taking the porch steps two at a time. "It looks like he got away."

She might have been able to convince herself that the traces of huskiness in his voice had to do with the silence of the late summer night, but try as she might, she couldn't dismiss the open longing in his eyes as easily. It rekindled old feelings deep inside her, old emotions and sentiments she thought she'd forgotten a long time ago.

For a moment it confused her. But as Luke slowly ambled closer, a knot formed in her stomach, her confusion giving way to more disturbing emotions. Worry and fear and anguish.

"Don't worry," he said, "we can try again tomorrow night."

"I don't think so, Luke."

The tone of Jillian's voice stopped Luke's forward motion. He didn't like the expression on her face or the way she was shaking her head. Her shoulders were squared, her chin set at a stubborn angle that could only mean trouble.

Waiting until his voice was composed, he said, "If you have plans tomorrow, we can do it the following night."

She shook her head again, but she didn't speak.

Before what little patience he possessed completely evaporated into thin air, he tried another tack. "We can't just let whoever did this get away with it."

She folded her arms and raised her chin another notch. "From now on I'm going to leave this up to the sheriff. In the meantime I won't put anything out here on the porch."

"Jillian, what's going on?"

She took a backward step and said, "I appreciate your help, but I think it would be best if you and I didn't see each other after office hours."

"Best for who?" he bellowed.

She ducked her head, then glanced at the dark houses all around. Luke didn't give a rip who heard him or who he woke up. In fact, he would have preferred to shout his intentions at the top of his lungs. But some semblance of rationality had him lowering his voice and moving closer.

"I don't believe you mean that, Jillian, not after what happened between us five minutes ago. Besides, I saved your life. And you know what that means."

He wasn't really surprised that she didn't dignify his remark with a reply, but he didn't expect her to move away from him so suddenly that he felt the flutter of a breeze in her wake. From the other side of the porch she said, "You know I'm not staying in Jasper Gulch."

"You're here now."

Shrugging, she said, "I can't imagine why you'd want to waste your time on me, knowing I'm only going to be here for a few more weeks, when there are four more single women moving to town tomorrow."

Luke felt a muscle working in his jaw. "Maybe I don't consider you a waste of my time."

"Seriously, Luke. Don't you think you should be looking for a woman to settle down with, a woman to share your life here in Jasper Gulch? You really should give someone else a chance."

He raked his fingers through his hair again, too exasperated to speak. Who could blame him? The one woman in all the world he ached to take in his arms was encouraging him, Luke Carson, to see other women.

He didn't want to see other women, dammit. He wanted to see *Jillian*.

This didn't make any sense. None of it. They'd shared something pretty darn incredible little more than five minutes ago. He'd imagined her kiss a hundred times, but the softly drawn breath she'd taken as she'd raised her face toward his hadn't come from one of his dreams. The attraction between them had been as real as the shadows of regret in her eyes right now.

That made him pause.

She really did look remorseful, sad almost.

"Jillian, what's wrong? What aren't you telling me?"

Her eyes darted to his, held, then slid away. "What makes you think something's wrong?"

Taking a step closer, he said, "Oh, I don't know. Maybe it has something to do with the fact that you look like you just lost your best friend."

She jerked back as if she'd been slapped. It confused Luke even more. Cupping the back of his neck with one hand, he kneaded the muscles knotted there. He'd never pretended to understand her, but tonight he was completely baffled.

She released the breath she'd been holding, the porch light catching in her eyes as she said, "I enjoyed hearing about your mother, Luke. I guess I'm a little sorry that I won't be here when she returns."

A pickup truck turned the corner, then slowly pulled to the curb out front. Lisa practically jumped out of the passenger-side door and called an extremely hasty goodbye to Boomer Brown. Another time Luke might have appreciated the humor in the situation, but tonight his brain felt fuzzy and he couldn't think of a thing to say.

Jillian, on the other hand, couldn't have been much clearer if she'd tried. She wasn't going to stay in Jasper Gulch, and there were no *ands, ifs* or *buts* about it. Fine. He didn't have to be hit over the head with the truth. He did have some pride, after all. Somewhere.

He turned on his heel and strode into the house, uncaring that the screen door banged shut behind him. He was back seconds later. With hat in hand he headed for the porch steps, nearly running over Lisa in the process.

He muttered a quick "Pardon me." And kept on going.

"What was that all about?"

Lisa and Jillian were both standing on the porch, staring at taillights as a second truck squealed around the corner in a matter of seconds. Jillian cast her friend a surreptitious glance, then said, "I was about to ask you the same question."

"Ugh!" was all Lisa would say concerning her date with Boomer.

With a slight shake of her head, Jillian said, "The thief got away again."

Raising delicately arched eyebrows, Lisa said, "Something tells me there was more to the severe expression on Luke Carson's face than a foiled stakeout."

Jillian brushed an imaginary speck of lint from her navy shorts. "As a matter of fact, there was."

"Are you going to tell me what it was?"

"I told him there weren't going to be any more stakeouts."

"Why did you do that?"

"Because," Jillian said, her eyes trained on the strap of her leather sandal. "I'm afraid he's getting the wrong idea about *us*."

"And why do you suppose that is?" Lisa asked.

"*Why* doesn't matter. What matters is that I've put an end to it, once and for all."

Jillian glanced up and found Lisa looking at her. Her lips were parted slightly, her eyes crinkled at the corners as if she wanted to say something but didn't know how. Quiet and withdrawn, she turned and went inside.

Jillian was left standing on the porch alone, torn by conflicting emotions. It wasn't like Lisa to keep her thoughts to herself, yet Jillian wasn't sure she wanted to hear what was on her friend's mind.

She went inside after a time, the sound of liquid pouring over crackling ice luring her into the kitchen. Lisa was facing the counter, her fingers curled around a tall glass of lemonade.

Jillian wandered around the room listlessly, toying with a kitchen towel, smoothing her hand along the counter. "You might as well say what's on your mind, Lisa."

Ice cubes jangled, and Lisa finally turned around. "You aren't going to like this, but Luke isn't the only one who has the wrong idea about the two of you."

Jillian turned her head so fast her hair swished to the front of one shoulder. "What do you mean?"

"Well, I wasn't going to say anything, but as far as I can tell, most of the area bachelors have scratched you off their lists because they think you and Luke are a couple."

"But Luke and I haven't gone anywhere together."

"It doesn't matter. Everyone knows you're working for him, and the little kiss you gave him in the middle of Main Street last week was all over town an hour after it happened. Add to that the fact that you haven't accepted a date with anyone else and, well, I guess the townspeople have put two and two together and have come up with what they believe is four."

Lisa must have read the horrified expression on Jillian's face accurately, because she said, "I'm only telling you what I've heard. These people, especially the men, think you and Luke are an item, plain and simple."

"But we're not. I just can't fall in love, Lisa. You know that."

"You don't have to explain your reasons to me, Jillian. I know your life story, remember? But I'd be lying if I told you I wasn't hoping that you'd change your mind, or that maybe one of the men out here would change it for you."

Jillian closed her eyes. Leaning against the edge of the counter, she couldn't blame Lisa for being honest. They'd been friends for a long, long time. In many ways they'd been closer than sisters. They both knew how it felt to be totally alone. They weren't close because of birth order or blood. They were close because they'd chosen to be friends. "For life," they'd always said. Forever.

She'd always known that leaving Lisa here in Jasper Gulch wasn't going to be easy. But falling in love would have been even harder. It would be wise to remember that. While she was at it, it would be wise to find a way to let the local bachelors know that she and Luke Carson were *not* a couple in any way, shape or form.

"You boys did a dandy job of planning the town picnic. Just dandy."

Luke was vaguely aware that Cletus McCully was looking him up and down, but he paid the old geezer about as much attention as he'd paid Isabell Pruitt the last time she'd tasted the punch to see if it was spiked. Cletus's scrutiny was annoying, but compared to the sight of Jillian being twirled around the floor by yet another bachelor, it was but a fly in the ointment.

Unaware or uncaring that he was being ignored, Cletus snapped his suspenders and rocked back on his heels. "I don't believe I've ever seen sorrier lookin' men in my life."

Wyatt made a sound deep in his throat and said, "Yeah, the way those boys are falling over themselves trying to impress the new women is enough to turn a person's stomach."

"I was referrin' to the three of you."

Three heads jerked Cletus's way. Three scowls deepened.

Luke clenched his teeth and shook his head. He, Wyatt and Clayt had fallen right into that one.

"You boys are doing a mighty fine job of holding up that there wall, too. That's boot-stompin' music. What I can't figure out is why you aren't out there dancin' with the single women."

Luke, Wyatt and Clayt exchanged looks, took turns shrugging and folded their arms at their chests. They all had their own reasons for *not* dancing, and apparently none of them felt like discussing them with Cletus.

By most people's standards, the town picnic would have been considered a success. After all, the citizens of Jasper Gulch really had thrown out the welcome mat to the new-comers. The festivities had started in the middle of the afternoon, beginning with a parade down Main Street. What the parade lacked in size, it more than made up for with the vigor of the high school's eighteen-piece marching band and a group of ripping, roaring rodeo riders who were all spiffed up for the occasion.

The parade ended at Cletus's property just south of town, where a roping contest was held. There had been three-legged races, Simon Says and water balloons for the kids, and a pie-eating contest for anyone wishing to participate. At five o'clock sharp the Ladies Aid Society had set out enough food to feed a small army. And the Anderson brothers had started tuning their guitars in the far corner of the barn around seven-thirty. Another time Luke might have appreciated the beat of the twangy country-western music. But not tonight.

As far as he could tell, every one of the county's sixty-two bachelors had shown up. Which was just about how many men Jillian had danced with so far.

Glowering, he clamped his mouth shut on a succinct cuss word. The only reason he knew he'd made a disparaging sound out loud was because Clayt, Wyatt and Cletus all turned to look at him.

A little skirmish caught their attention, saving him from having to explain. Two boys who couldn't have been more than ten years old were poking fun at a skinny little girl whose hair was tied up with a lopsided ribbon.

Clayt moved forward like a shot.

Cletus's gnarled hand stopped him in his tracks. "Wait up, there, boy. Let's give Haley a chance to hold her own with those rascals."

Haley's chin quivered and her eyes glistened. Luke wouldn't have been the least bit surprised if his niece had burst into tears. Instead she sucked in her lower lip and popped the first boy a good one in the stomach.

The boy doubled over. With eyes as round as saucers, his friend turned on his heel and darted off into the crowd. Luckily Clayt was able to restrain the other urchin who came up spitting mad, his fists raised for battle. It was Cletus who grasped Haley by the shoulders before she managed to place the second blow. He wasn't, however, able to curb the argument taking place between the two children.

"Did not."

"Did so."

"Did not."

"Wanna bet?"

"Yeah!"

"Jeremy," Cletus admonished, "didn't anyone ever teach you not to pick on girls?"

"She started it!"

"Did not."

"Did so."

"Only because you had it coming," Haley declared, changing tactics.

Luke supposed he shouldn't have been surprised by his niece's behavior. She was a Carson, after all. If the grass stains on her knees and the dirt smudges on her face weren't proof enough, her belligerent attitude would have given her away any day of the week.

"Did you start it?" Clayt asked his little girl.

For the first time Haley seemed to realize that she had an audience. She cast a glance all around, her gaze suddenly trained on the toe of her dusty shoe.

Luke's heart went out to the poor kid. At nine years old she was at that awkward age—too old for dolls but too young for boys. Until now Haley hadn't lived with her father since she was two years old. Even on weekend visits Clayt had never pretended to know how to handle his own daughter. Luke wondered what he was going to do about the situation this time.

"I think you should apologize," Clayt declared.

The child was shaking her head before he'd finished speaking.

"Haley," he said, drawing her name out as long as it could go.

"Do I hafta?"

"Yes, you have to."

The girl shrugged Cletus's hands off her shoulders. Then, in a voice smaller than she was, she said, "Sorry."

Jeremy Everts looked shocked and duly dumbfounded. He mumbled something under his breath, then dazedly turned and walked away. Wyatt, Cletus and Clayt were so busy exchanging relieved glances they didn't see Haley stick her tongue out at Jeremy's retreating back.

Luke's smile practically cracked his face, but glimpsing Haley's feistiness was worth the discomfort. That little kid might have been sad and disillusioned, but she wasn't completely beaten, not by a long shot.

Clayt went down on one knee to confer with his daughter. A few minutes later Haley ambled away forlornly. Watching her go, Luke asked, "Did she tell you why she hit him?"

While the Anderson brothers persecuted a song about "boot-scootin' boogey," Clayt nodded. "They said Victoria dumped her on my doorstep because she doesn't want her."

Suddenly Luke wasn't sorry that Haley had hit the brat. He would have done the same thing at that age. Who did Jeremy Everts think he was, saying a thing like that? Never mind that it was true. Eyeing his brother, Luke said, "It looks as if your daughter is getting her spunk back."

Clayt shook his head. "Maybe. But I'm still worried. She's been lethargic, and I swear she doesn't eat enough to keep a bird alive. She's a tough kid, but she misses Victoria. I guess a bad mother is better than no mother at all."

"Horse feathers!" Cletus crowed. "Clayton, what that little girl of yours needs is a mother, all right, but not necessarily one who's blood related. She needs a woman who'll put her first. If you won't dance with my granddaughter, get your rear end out there and ask one of the new gals to dance. Wyatt and Luke, that goes double for you. After all, there's only so much one old man can do. Now go on, before the lines get any longer."

Wyatt and Clayt shared a long look and a longer shrug. When they were good and ready, they set off across the barn to do as Cletus said. Luke stayed where he was, watching.

Ben Jacobs marched past, doing a stiff version of a country line dance. Luke's gaze narrowed on the woman at his side.

Jillian was wearing a straight denim skirt and matching shirt with white fringe just below the shoulders and around the hem, and white cowboy boots, no less. He didn't have a problem with her outfit. His problem was with the way practically every other man in the room was looking at that danged fringe.

"Well?" Cletus declared. "What's takin' you so long?"

The lights he and Wyatt had strung beneath the rafters earlier that morning glinted off Jillian's red hair, shooting it with gold and amber and bronze. When those same lights touched upon the smile she gave Ben, Luke bit back a curse.

"Well?" Cletus prodded. "What do ya have to say for yourself?"

Pulling the brim of his black hat lower over his eyes, Luke shook his head.

"Then go on. Get in line."

"That's just it, Cletus. I don't stand in line."

"Well, you'd better do something, or one of those bachelors is gonna beat you to the punch."

Cletus ambled away on his skinny bowed legs as if the situation was hopeless. Luke stayed where he was, wondering if it really was. He sure hadn't gotten any closer to Jillian in the days since that confounded stakeout. In fact, he'd rarely seen her. She'd kept her distance in the office. Even when he spoke to her from the truck phone, she'd maintained a curtness and professionalism that had been impossible to penetrate.

It was almost as if that kiss had never happened.

But it had happened. She'd raised her face and met him halfway. And then she'd proceeded to practically melt beneath his touch. So what in the hell was going on?

When the song ended, Luke was still searching for a plausible explanation. By the time that tenderfoot Jason Tucker had claimed Jillian's next dance, Luke had come up with one.

Whether she admitted it or not, she *had* responded to that kiss. A person didn't act as if it had never happened unless she was trying to believe it herself. The question was, Why?

Why would she pretend that they'd never kissed? And why would she be making it a point to dance with every bachelor who asked? Who was she trying to convince? Everyone else? Or herself?

Maybe it was high time he found out.

While he was trying to decide how to do that, the people

in the center of the floor stepped backward instead of forward; others went right instead of left. By the time the song ended, there was mass confusion on the dance floor. Jason Tucker didn't seem to know where Jillian had gone. But Luke's eyes had trailed her into the shadows underneath the hayloft and on out the door.

He strode through the door closest to him, sidestepping a couple of kids playing tag in the dark. The sky was teasing them with heat lightning again, but it was the flash of white fringe over by the corral that caught his attention.

"Nice night."

Jillian didn't have to turn around to see who had spoken. She would have recognized Luke's low, smooth voice anywhere. It did crazy things to her breathing, not to mention her peace of mind.

Shoring her heart against the effect he had on her, she calmly, politely said, "It looks as if your picnic turned out to be a success."

His boots creaked slightly, letting her know that he'd taken a step or two closer. "You've certainly done your share to ensure that everyone has a good time."

She swung around the instant she heard the note of censure in his voice. His eyes were shaded by his hat, but although his jaw was set in a firm line, he didn't appear to be overly angry. Deciding it must have been her imagination or a guilty conscience, she forced herself to relax. After all, she had no reason to feel guilty. The fact that she and Luke had kissed didn't make her his any more than the fact that he saved her life did. *Forget about that kiss.* She closed her eyes, then smoothed a few stray locks of hair behind her ear. "I probably should be getting back inside."

"Jillian, wait."

She stopped in her tracks despite her resolve not to. Turning slowly, she said, "What do you want, Luke?"

Luke was glad his eyes were in shadow so she couldn't see the yearning in them. "I don't necessarily want anything, Jillian."

"You don't?"

Heat lightning shimmered across the horizon at the same time he shook his head. *Liar.* "We've both been so busy all week I haven't seen much of you." It was a good thing it was only heat lightning and not the real thing, or he might have been struck down where he stood.

Glancing around, he said, "It was nice of Cletus to let us have the picnic at his place, don't you think?"

She looked a little surprised at his complimentary attitude toward Cletus. Not that Luke blamed her. He didn't normally sing the old man's praises. But what the heck. Desperate situations called for desperate measures.

Motioning to the small, clapboard house in the distance, he said, "I sure spent a lot of time in that house when I was a kid."

"In Cletus's house? Why?"

"Didn't I ever tell you that Cletus raised Wyatt and Mel?"

At the slow shake of her head, he said, "Their folks drowned when a flash flood took out the bridge they were trying to cross over the Bad River."

Luke and Jillian turned their head as three children streaked by. In a voice that was noticeably softer, she asked, "How old was Melody?"

"Five or six."

Making a sad, mourning kind of sound, she looked directly into his eyes for the first time all night. "Would you tell me something, Luke?"

His heart thudded and his breathing deepened, along with his thoughts. Tipping the rim of his hat up with two fingers, he thought, *This is more like it.* He took a few steps toward a shelterbelt of trees, waiting to make sure she followed before he asked, "What would you like to know?"

"I'm curious about something. That ad luring women to Jasper Gulch said there are sixty-two bachelors and only six marriageable women. I can understand how the men might think that Isabell Pruitt, Mertyl Gentry and maybe even DoraLee Sullivan are a little too old for them. And I suppose Brandy Schafer and Tracy Gentry are a little too young. What I don't understand is why nobody is pursuing Melody McCully. She's pretty and independent and *just the right age.*"

"It doesn't matter."

"What do you mean it doesn't matter?" she asked.

"She hasn't been out with one of the locals in almost ten years."

"But why?"

He waited to answer until after they stopped walking, until after he turned to face her. "For a long time she wouldn't go. And now they've stopped asking."

"Why wouldn't she go out with any of them?"

"Because she's had a crush on Clayt since she was twelve years old."

"Your brother Clayt?"

"The one and only."

Luke enjoyed the incredulous expression on Jillian's face. Not because he took satisfaction in confusing her, but because of the way her lips parted in the most enticing way.

"Are you sure?" she asked.

"Of course I'm sure."

"How do you know?"

"Everyone knows."

"Does Melody know that everybody knows?" she asked.

"Probably, although she'll deny it if you ask her outright."

Jillian could barely believe what she was hearing. She and Luke were standing in the shadows, strains of twangy music wafting from the barn. Farther away a group of children were playing hide-and-seek near the house, and a hundred yards in the opposite direction some old-timers were enjoying smelly cigars and sips from a small silver flask behind Cletus's shed. It was just an ordinary hot July night during a town picnic that was slowly winding down. There was really no reason for the subtle softening around her heart, or for the memory of one long, dreamy kiss to slip into her thoughts.

Resigning herself to the fact that she probably wasn't going to be able to forget that kiss, she glanced up at Luke. "If all the men in Jasper Gulch are as overconfident as you are, it's no wonder they're still single."

"I'm not overconfident, Jillian." His voice had dipped so low it sounded more like an echo than a whisper.

"You're not?" she whispered back, wondering why none of the other men she'd talked to tonight had had this effect on her senses.

He shook his head. "If I was, I wouldn't be talking right now."

She knew she shouldn't, but she couldn't stop herself from asking, "What would you be doing?"

"This." He leaned closer, bringing his mouth down to hers in a featherlight kiss. His lips were surprisingly gentle, unbelievably persuasive, undeniably tantalizing. Her eyes drifted shut, and she kissed him back with a hunger that had a way of coming to life when she least expected. His hands cupped her shoulders, his fingers trailing through the fringe, drawing her closer.

Heat emanated from his entire body, warming her in ways only a man could warm a woman. There was a tingle in the pit of her stomach, a jolt in her heart and a pounding at her pulse points. As his mouth worked its own brand of magic over hers, she melted against him. She wasn't shocked at her eager response, or his, but as the kiss meandered across her senses, she knew she had to do something to stop it before it was too late.

She turned her head slightly. His mouth left hers, only to press a whisper-soft kiss near her ear.

"Ah, Jillian, I don't think you know how much I've been aching to do that all night. Let's go someplace where we can be alone."

There it was again, that husky entreaty in his voice that all but erased every rational thought in her head.

"I can't, Luke."

"Yes you can. All you have to do is leave with me right now."

She glanced around, suddenly remembering that although they were in the shadows they weren't alone. Now that Luke had told her how these people wouldn't let Melody forget one childhood crush, she understood why it had been so difficult for them to believe that she and Luke weren't a couple. What she didn't like was the fact that it was so difficult for *her* to believe that they weren't.

"What will everyone think if they see us like this?"

"Do you really care what these people think, Jillian?"

Her answer was slow in coming. "Not for my sake, but for yours, yes, I guess I do care."

Luke's hands fell away from her shoulders slowly. He wondered if she realized what she'd said. She cared about him. She might not have admitted it to herself, but she'd whispered it to him. The knowledge did amazing things to him, puffing his chest, swelling his head, making him grin. Hot damn. The woman was incredible. And she cared about him.

He wanted to raise his face to the sky and let loose a yee-ha that would let everyone know how good he felt. Before he could carry out his wish, she started back toward the barn.

"Where are you going?"

Her arms were crossed in front of her, her chin turned away from him. "Home."

"Home to Madison? Or home to Elm Street?" he asked, hurrying to catch up.

"To Elm Street."

"I'll give you a ride."

"There's no need for you to leave the party."

"I want to."

A woman's laughter carried to their ears. Glancing in the direction it had come from, Jillian said, "I can't let you do that, Luke. Do you see that woman over there talking to Lisa? Her name is Brittany Matthews. She and her five-year-old daughter just moved here all the way from New Jersey two days ago."

Luke wondered what that had to do with him, but looked over at the woman just to be polite.

"I talked to her earlier. She was an office manager back in New Jersey, and I was just thinking that since my stay here is only temporary, maybe you should talk to her about working for you."

Luke felt his chin drop and his temper rise. "You can still say your stay here is only temporary after kissing me as if there's no tomorrow?"

"That shouldn't have happened. And there will be a tomorrow, Luke."

He muttered a short, succinct cuss word that was completely unbecoming and ungentlemanly but extremely eloquent under the circumstances. He would have liked to utter a few more, but she cast him a look of understanding that kept him quiet.

"I'm not here to find a husband, Luke. Lisa is."

Lisa chose that moment to glance their way. Evidently noting the tense atmosphere surrounding them, she walked on over and said, "Is everything all right, Jillian?"

Jillian nodded. "I was just going to ask you if I could borrow your car keys."

"You're going home?" Lisa asked, glancing from Jillian to Luke and back again.

At Jillian's second nod, she said, "Of course you can borrow my keys. I'll catch a ride home with Brittany or one of the bachelors. Hold on, I'll go in and get my purse."

"No, Lisa, that's okay," Jillian said quickly. "I know where they are." Without another word, she set off toward the barn, leaving Luke and Lisa staring after her.

Luke's anger made its presence known from his head to his toes. Seething, he said, "I can't figure out what kind of game she's playing."

Lisa waited to speak until after Jillian disappeared inside the barn. "Do you really believe a woman like Jillian would play games with a man's heart, Luke?"

For the first time Luke took a long, hard look at Lisa Markman. She wasn't quite as tall as Jillian, her hair dark instead of red, her eyes a deep shade of brown. He supposed she was beautiful in her own right, but it wasn't her beauty he was looking at in the depths of her eyes. It was his own reflection, and it made him uncomfortable, because he didn't especially like what he saw.

Lisa was right. Jillian wasn't *playing* anything. She was serious. Heart-wrenching, gut-clenching, show-stopping serious.

"I don't understand her," he said with all the honesty he possessed. "Why would she choose a job over the opportunity to love and be loved in return?"

Lisa's stare didn't waver, and although she didn't utter a word, her eyes said plenty.

"What's she afraid of, Lisa?"

The dark-haired woman still didn't answer. But she didn't have to. A few things about Jillian were beginning to make sense. She was fiercely loyal, kind and giving and protective. He'd bet his practice that she would love with an even greater intensity.

That's when it dawned on him.

She wasn't running to a job. She was running away.

"Who hurt her, Lisa?"

"I'd rather not say."

Luke felt his eyes narrow. "All right. Tell me this. Was it her husband?"

"No."

"Her fiancé?"

Heaving a great sigh, Lisa said, "He was more than her fiancé. He was her best friend."

Luke felt as if he'd been kicked in the chest. "What happened?"

"Brian died five years ago."

Brian. His name was Brian. The knowledge shot through Luke like gunfire. He remembered the expression that had crossed Jillian's face after their stakeout, when he'd told her she looked like she'd just lost her best friend. A knot rose to his throat, and a muscle worked in his jaw, because now he knew that she had. Jealousy, green and ugly, reared up inside him. Earlier he'd told Cletus he didn't stand in line. How in the hell was he supposed to cut in front of a ghost?

Swallowing, he asked, "What was he like?"

Lisa glanced back toward the barn where Jillian was quickly making her way toward them, keys in hand. Keeping her gaze averted, she said, "I'm not sure Jillian's put it together yet, but I noticed the resemblance right away."

"The resemblance?" Luke asked.

"To you."

Luke tried to speak, but couldn't. Lisa seemed to understand. Casting him a smile warm enough to slice through butter, she nodded and set off to tell Jillian goodbye.

Luke watched the interaction between the two friends, using the brief interlude to get his thoughts in order. Within seconds, Lisa was heading for the barn once again,

and Jillian was on her way toward the field where rows of
cars and trucks were parked.

"Jillian, wait."

He fell into step beside her and was surprised when she
immediately began talking. "Now that you've talked to
Lisa, what do you think of her?"

Fitting his stride to hers, he said, "I can see why you're
friends."

She nodded, and although it was dark, he was pretty
sure he saw her small smile. "Then there shouldn't be any
problem."

"Problem?"

"With you asking her out."

Luke almost croaked. "Pardon me?"

"You practically admitted that you like her. And she's
gorgeous."

"Are you trying to tell me you want me to date your
best friend?"

His voice was more of a growl, but it stopped her in
her tracks. Turning slowly, she said, "I think that's a wonderful idea."

"Now just a cotton-picking minute."

"What?" she asked, as innocent as could be.

A slow heat crawled up Luke's neck. Any second now
steam was going to shoot out of his ears. He wanted to
groan out loud because, dammit, he'd walked right into
that one.

Jillian wanted him to *date* her best friend? How in the
world could she, after the way she'd kissed him, after the
way she'd responded to him? Hell, she'd practically melted
in his arms. She cared about him, but she was too gawd-
blain stubborn to admit it to herself. He'd never known
another woman like her. He'd sure as heck never known
one who *wanted* him to see other women. No. The women
in his life had always been the jealous type.

He stopped short. Ideas formed, one after another. He

wanted her. She wanted him. And yet she claimed she wanted him to date her best friend. Well, maybe it was high time he gave them both what they wanted.

He took one long-legged step, angling her his best killer grin. She eyed him warily and took a step back.

He took another. And so did she. So it went, until her back was against a sawhorse marking the first row of vehicles.

He moved in closer, closer. Letting his gaze roam her features, he took in her wide blue eyes and pale skin and reached his hand toward her, smoothing an errant strand of hair from her cheek.

In a voice echoing with longing, he said, "Maybe you're right, Jillian. Maybe it is time I got to know your beautiful friend."

He saw the surprise in her eyes, and when her gaze dropped to his mouth, he saw the need. Using every ounce of willpower he possessed, he let his fingers trail through the wispy strands of hair at her temple then removed his hand and took a backward step.

"Do you mean it?" she asked. "Do you really want to get to know Lisa?"

"Sure. Why not?"

"Do you want me to set it up?"

He shook his head once. "This isn't junior high. In case you haven't noticed, I'm a man. And I'm perfectly capable of arranging my own dates."

"Oh. Of course."

Leaning toward her, he kissed her cheek, surprising the living daylights out of her, and out of him. Straightening, he tipped his hat, turned on his heel and strode away.

Chapter Seven

Jillian shifted on the bar stool and crossed her legs. Listening with only one ear to the conversation between two of her newest friends, she took a sip of soda and glanced around. There wasn't much going on in town, not even at the Crazy Horse. Evidently everyone had worn themselves out at the town picnic yesterday and had decided not to venture far from home tonight.

She'd begun her evening at the diner, hugging the back of the room until the last customer finally left. After helping Melody close up for the night, the two of them had decided to stop in and say hello to DoraLee Sullivan, the sole proprietor of the Crazy Horse Saloon. That had been an hour ago, an hour in which DoraLee had practically talked their ears off in between serving drinks to the Sunday night-regulars at the other end of the bar and a group of old-timer's playing poker at a table near the back of the room.

So far Jillian had learned that DoraLee ''poured a mean drink,'' and that her husband, Delbert, had died ten years ago after being thrown from a bucking bronco. Plunking an open bottle of whiskey in front of her, DoraLee patted her coiffed bottle-blond hair and eyed Jillian.

"Delbert's daddy owned the saloon before him. After Del died, it seemed only natural that I take it over."

Continuing in a quieter voice, she said, "I don't know how much Mel, here, has told you about me and Delbert..."

Jillian cast Melody a sidelong glance, wondering where the conversation was headed. With a mild shake of her head, she said, "I don't think Melody's much of a gossip, DoraLee, because she hasn't uttered a word about you and your late husband."

DoraLee winked one well made-up eye and smiled at the two younger women. "You're right. Our Mel has never had much use for gossip, so you're gonna hear about Delbert and me straight from the horse's mouth. My Delbert had coal black hair and sky blue eyes. What he lacked in height, he more than made up for with his well-defined muscles and pure cowboy brawn. Everybody, including me, knew he had an eye for the ladies, just as we all knew he messed around with the rodeo bunnies from time to time."

"Oh, DoraLee," Jillian whispered, "I'm so sorry."

"So am I, sugar. So am I. It's easy for people to say they would have thrown him out on his ear, and maybe a lot of women would have, ya know?"

Jillian made a sympathetic sound and reached for the glass of soda in front of her, thinking she wasn't a good one to talk about such matters, not when the man who could turn her knees to jelly was out with her best friend this very minute.

She and Melody shared a long look in the mirror behind the bar. Melody McCully was almost thirty years old, but she looked younger. Although Jillian had seen the prettiness in the other woman's features the first time they met, she'd instinctively realized that it wasn't the kind of beauty that flashed like a neon sign. Melody's features had the kind of symmetry and wholesomeness a person noticed a little at a time. Her hair, a dark shade of blond, hung down her back in a loose braid. Her eyes were pale blue, her mouth equally prone to smiling and frowning. There wasn't much to her, but she was no weakling. Jillian had seen firsthand the way she could wield a broom in the diner and hoist chairs to the top of a table as if they were made of bamboo instead of hardened oak.

"Mel, honey," DoraLee crooned, "is your friend always this quiet, or does she have something on her mind?"

"I don't know, DoraLee. Why don't you ask her?"

DoraLee released a huff of air through her nose and shook her head. Placing one hand on her ample hip, she looked at Jillian and said, "Well? Are you gonna make me ask?"

Jillian waited to answer until after she'd traced an *L* in the condensation on the side of her glass. "Have you ever been thoroughly confused, DoraLee?"

"Sugar, I've been thoroughly confused most of my life. But if you think it's bad now, just wait. The closer you get to fifty, the harder it's gonna be to tell an honest-to-goodness feeling from a mood swing. What're you confused about?"

One by one, tiny beads of water distorted the initial Jillian had traced onto her glass. Following one droplet's journey to the bottom, she thought, *Luke,* but whispered, "Life."

DoraLee made a tsk, tsk, tsk sound and shook her head. "Sugar, trying to figure out life is about as futile as trying to figure out a man. Both will give you wrinkles and gray hair faster than anything else, but neither will ever become crystal clear. It just so happens that I know the perfect cure for what ails you."

Without another word, the voluptuous bleached blonde set about gathering supplies, which consisted of shot glasses, a salt shaker, slices of lemon and a tall bottle of tequila. She was extremely meticulous about the way she filled the small glasses, then replaced the bottle's cap. When she had everything in order, she wet the skin on the back of her hand and quickly sprinkled it with salt. Raising her hand to her lips, she said, "Girls, follow my lead."

DoraLee licked the salt from her hand with her pink tongue. By the time she'd tossed the shot of tequila back, her cheeks were pink, too. She sucked on the lemon with her eyes shut, and when she spoke again, her voice had lowered an entire octave.

"Well?" she asked, opening her eyes with quiet emphasis.

Jillian was a little surprised when Melody reached for the salt shaker, but someone could have knocked her over with a feather when she did the same thing.

The salt left a strange, bitter taste in her mouth, but it was nothing compared to the fire that burned a path down her throat or the explosion the tequila made when it hit the pit of her stomach. She gasped for air, accepting the lemon DoraLee was pushing into her hand. Sputtering, eyes watering, she lowered the lemon rind to the bar and met the older woman's beam of approval.

"Feel any better?" DoraLee asked.

Melody closed her eyes and covered her mouth. "I think I'm going to throw up."

Jillian didn't know what to do about the funny shade of green Melody's face had turned, but DoraLee sprang into action, holding a pretzel to Melody's lips and crooning, "Take a bite of this. It'll calm your churning stomach."

Pale-faced and bleary-eyed, Melody nibbled on a corner, chewed, then nibbled on another.

"Shoot, sugar, I didn't mean to make you sick."

Finishing the pretzel, Melody said, "It isn't your fault, DoraLee. I've been feeling sick ever since Clayt came up with the idea of advertising for women to come to Jasper Gulch.''

She shot a glance at both Jillian and DoraLee, a blush climbing to her cheeks. Quickly she averted her gaze to the floor, as if she wanted to crawl in a knothole and pull it in after her. In a voice thick with both tequila and apology, she said, "Not that I haven't enjoyed making new friends, and all. But what am I? Chopped liver?"

Jillian was amazed at what she was hearing. Luke was right. Melody McCully really did have feelings for Clayt Carson. From the sound of things they were nothing new.

"There, there," DoraLee crooned to Melody. "Clayton Carson is as blind as a bat if he can't see what's been right in front of his face all along. But at least your color's starting to improve. You'll be feeling as good as new in no time at all."

"Thanks, DoraLee," Melody murmured.

"No need to thank me, sugar. This is what friends are for. It's why women seek out other women. Don't you wonder why we spend so much time and energy pining away after men, when it's our female friends we turn to in times of need?"

She winked at Jillian and said, "You didn't do bad at all with that shot of tequila. I'll make sure Melody gets back to her place safe and sound. Now why don't you go on home and wait for your friend to come in from her date with that other heartbreaking Carson brother."

If Jillian's throat hadn't been burning from the tequila, she would have gasped. Amazed and slightly shaken, she glanced from DoraLee to Melody and back again, slowly coming to the conclusion that there was no sense wondering how they could have possibly known how horrible she was feeling about Lisa and Luke's date. The two other women gave her an affectionate, companionable smile. Jillian smiled back, thinking they made quite a threesome, their throats all raspy, their eyes all watery, their hearts all lying wide open for all to see.

"What about you, DoraLee?" Jillian finally asked "Who's going to make sure you get home safe and secure?"

"Me? I'm a tough old bird. Don't you worry about me. I'll be just fine."

"Do you know what I think?" Jillian asked, sliding from the stool.

"What, sugar?"

"I think you're a lot softer than you want us to believe."

DoraLee dabbed at her nose with a paper napkin and said, "Go on, get out of here. And Jillian? I'd appreciate it if you'd keep that particular observation to yourself."

From the next bar stool, Melody said, "And I'd appreciate it if you wouldn't mention anything about the little slip I made about Clayt."

Jillian pretended to turn a lock at the corner of her mouth. With a sad sort of smile, she headed for the door thinking that they were probably crazy if they thought there was a snowball's chance in July that the fine folks of Jasper Gulch didn't know exactly what was going on. This was a small town. Actually, it was smaller than small. Gossip had a way of spreading from one corner to the other faster than water could soak into a dry sponge.

After casting one last look at her two new friends at the bar, she did as DoraLee suggested, stepping out into the dark night and slowly heading home. The wind blew in from the plains, dusty and dry. It trailed through the loose strands of her hair and pressed her loose-fitting skirt to her thighs. One thing it didn't do was cool her warm skin.

Or take her mind off the mess she'd gotten her emotions into.

She was still amazed that DoraLee had somehow known how sick Jillian felt about the fact that her best friend was out with Luke this very minute. What DoraLee had no way of knowing was that *she'd* suggested it.

Jillian's stomach burned from the tequila, but it didn't ache half as much as the jealousy cutting through her or the guilt stinging like salt in an open wound. Luke was out with her best friend. And she had no one to blame but herself.

Was that a truck she heard?

Jillian jumped to her feet before she could stop herself.

Yes, that was most definitely a truck. And those were definitely two doors clicking shut out in the quiet street in front of the house.

Lisa and Luke were back.

Forcing herself to sit back down, she picked up a magazine she'd bought a few days ago, opened the front cover and automatically began leafing through the pages. Unfortunately, the image swimming inside her head wasn't one of a brightly colored advertisement for perfume or makeup, but of a dark-haired woman raising her face toward a man wearing a black cowboy hat.

She rubbed a hand across her eyes, trying to dispel the image just as she'd done a hundred times before. To no avail. Oh, for heaven's sake. She was hopeless.

She'd arrived back at Lisa's rented house an hour and ten minutes ago. The longest hour and ten minutes she'd ever lived through. She'd meandered through the nearly dark house, lost in thought. With the clock ticking slowly, she'd stood in the doorway of each of the five rooms, wishing for some way to take her mind off the thoughts that were driving her to distraction.

She didn't know how it had happened, but in the two short weeks she'd known Luke, all the stone barricades she'd erected around her heart had slowly, surely turned into quicksand. She had feelings for Luke Carson. Strong feelings. Warm, hazy, dreamy feelings. She hadn't planned to let this happen. In fact, she'd been certain she could keep it from ever happening again. And yet here she was, sitting in a quiet house in the middle of a quiet town, her heart brimming with quiet emotions that simply refused to be ignored. These emotions scared her. They had since the first moment she'd looked into Luke's gray eyes. Subconsciously she'd known she was going to have to face them sooner or later.

She'd been facing them for an hour and ten minutes.

Earlier she'd paused in the bathroom doorway while she'd considered taking a shower, thinking that perhaps the warm water would wash away the panic deep inside. Knowing it would be futile, she'd wandered to the next room. And the next. She'd finally turned on the porch light, the light over the stove, and the one next to her grandfather's rocking chair where she'd decided to end her wait and face the truth.

The truth was she *cared* about Luke Carson. She *liked* him the way only a woman could like a man. It left her feeling at once vibrant and alive and as wobbly as the day-old kittens DoraLee had shown her in the Crazy Horse's back room.

For years Jillian had blocked these emotions from her existence, telling herself she was better off without them. Friendship and honorable goals made life worth living. For a long time she'd set off to prove it was so. For a long time it had been.

But then she'd met Luke. And tiny atoms had pinged off the invisible force field surrounding her. In a matter of a few short weeks those atoms had found a weakness in her armor, squeezing through to the very center of her, filling her with something very close to hope, something that could turn into love.

Lord, it felt sweet. But with the sweetness came fear. Of losing again. Of hurting. Again. But what terrified her even more than the aching or the losing or the hurting was the feeling that she was powerless. She'd had no control over a good share of her life, not her father's leaving, not her mother's death or her grandfather's. Certainly not Brian's. Jillian wasn't certain she could live through that kind of helplessness again. But could she live the rest of her life without these warm, shimmery emotions, now that she'd experienced them again?

She heard another hollow thud out on the porch, followed by footsteps. She stared at the picture window on the other side of the room, but from her vantage point, she couldn't see a thing, not even a shadow. Part of her was glad. If she actually saw Lisa and Luke kissing, she didn't know what she would do.

So she waited in silence. Her heart didn't pound in her ears, the rocking chair didn't creak, and no more sounds came from the porch.

What could possibly be taking Lisa so long to come inside?

Jillian's stomach roiled, her imagination working overtime. She tried to tell herself her nausea was the result of the tequila. But when the sound of two voices, one sultry and feminine, the other a quiet, dusky baritone, reached to her ears through the screen door, she knew she was lying to herself.

She loved Lisa, and she truly wanted her to find happiness. Luke and Lisa were both warm, volatile and lonely. They could very well be perfect for each other. She only wished the thought didn't make her heart ache through and through.

Give me strength, she prayed. Strength to do what's right, what's best. Strength to feel real happiness for Lisa if her date with Luke works out. And the strength to hide my own feelings and emotions.

The door opened ever so slowly. Shoring up her heart against what she was about to see, Jillian watched. And waited. It wasn't easy to think clearly with all the beats her heart was skipping, but after a few seconds she finally came to a startling realization. Lisa was alone.

Her best friend sauntered in, a small smile on her mouth—a mouth that very well could have been thoroughly kissed moments earlier. Swallowing the lump in her throat, Jillian said, "So, how was it? Your date, I mean."

"It was wonderful."

Lisa stretched like a cat, sensuous, sleek. Sickening.

Suddenly, Jillian wished she'd gone to bed. All the shoring up in the world couldn't have prepared her heart for what Lisa was about to say.

"Luke and I have so much in common."

Jillian's heart tipped slightly, then slowly sank into her stomach. She chastised herself, calling herself every horrible name she could think of. This was what she wanted for her friend. This was the reason she'd come with her out here to South Dakota. Lisa's childhood had been worse than Jillian's. A lot worse. She deserved a man like Luke, a man with stubborn tendencies and killer smiles, a man who could be arrogant one minute and beguiling the next, a man who could kiss a woman senseless any day of the week.

Her gaze strayed to Lisa's mouth. *Had Luke kissed her or hadn't he?*

Lisa twirled around so agilely her red skirt swished softly, stirring up a current of air. "You were right about everything, Jillian. Luke Carson is truly amazing."

He'd kissed her.

Why wouldn't he? Lisa was beautiful and brash and playful and nice. There probably wasn't a man on the planet who wouldn't want to kiss her. And Luke was definitely all man.

Of course he'd kissed her.

Envy dropped like lead to Jillian's stomach, eating a hole through her composure more surely than the tequila had. Oh, she was a horrible friend. Why in the world did Lisa even like her?

"You told me a lot about Luke," Lisa was saying, "but you never mentioned his sense of humor. I don't remember the last time I've laughed so hard. He's quite a talker, too, isn't he? We went to dinner in Pierre, and we must have talked for hours."

"That's nice, Lisa," Jillian said, pushing a lump back down her throat. It wasn't easy to plaster a smile on her face, but she did it, despite the fact that her lips hurt, her eyes hurt, her head hurt. Her heart hurt more than anything else. "I'm awfully tired tonight. How about if you tell me all about your date in the morning."

"Don't you want to know what we talked about?"

Jillian wanted to cry. Rising to her feet, she meandered to the stairs where she trailed her hand over the worn railing. Doing everything in her power to hold on to what was left of her composure, she said, "Ivy always says a person can sleep anytime. Of course, tell me what you and, um, er, Luke talked about."

"You."

Jillian's head jerked around so fast it was amazing she didn't give herself whiplash. "What?"

"We talked about you."

Without another word Lisa sashayed up the stairs. Jillian watched her turn around at the top, the sparkle in her dark eyes visible all the way from here.

"Whether you know it or not, Jillian, I'm not the only person in this town who thinks the world of you."

"You're not?"

The tiny shake of Lisa's head cast part of her face in shadow, delineating the gentle curve of her smile, which sent tears to Jillian's eyes. She doubted she deserved a friend like Lisa Markman, but there was one thing she had to know.

"Did Luke arrange for another date?"

"Of course not. And he won't, either, not when the person he can't get out of his mind is you."

At Jillian's horrified expression, Lisa rushed on. "But that's okay, Jillian. Luke's funny and warm and great to look at, but I'm afraid there's no chemistry between us. Can you say the same?"

Jillian felt as if all the blood was draining out of her face. Swallowing, she shook her head.

"That's what I thought. You must have a lot on your mind. Why don't you go out to the porch. Maybe the fresh air will help you put everything in perspective."

Jillian didn't know how long she stood at the bottom of the stairs, gazing into the shadows where Lisa had been. A minute or two or five. When she finally came out of her daze, one thought, and one thought alone, was playing through her mind like a song.

Luke and Lisa had talked about her. Her. Jillian Gabrielle Daniels.

She wondered what they'd said.

She considered marching straight upstairs and bothering Lisa with questions until she gave in and answered. But first she had to answer a few questions of her own. Was she strong enough to explore what was happening between her and Luke? Was she brave enough to take a chance on love again?

Doing as Lisa had suggested, she slipped outside, lost in thought. She ended her wandering on the steps, where she leaned against the railing, one hand tucked around her waist, the other twirling a stray lock of her hair.

Luke liked her. She knew it was true. He'd shown her in a hundred different ways. Why did the knowledge fill her with so many airy hopes and dreams she thought she'd buried a long time ago? More important, what was she going to do about them?

A sound, barely discernible above the whisper of the

prairie wind, reached her ears. She turned her head slowly, her gaze touching upon a dusty black Stetson and Luke Carson's weathered gray eyes.

Luke stood statue still, his back against the house, one knee bent, the heel of his boot hooked on a ridge in the siding. Jillian was looking at him, the light doing amazing things to her hair, burnishing it with the colors of some of man's most precious raw materials: copper, bronze and gold. She was wearing another airy wraparound skirt that hugged her hips and stirred his senses. Her feet were bare, which meant her legs were, too, which only served to heat his thoughts even more. He spent an inordinate amount of time staring at the loose bow tied at the side of her waist, wondering how much of a tug it would take to have the soft fabric pooling at her feet. He'd never much cared what a woman wore underneath her clothes, but the thought of what Jillian was, or wasn't, wearing underneath hers had his pulses pounding like war drums.

"Luke."

It was all she said, but it was enough to tempt him to march straight to her and lift her off her feet and put an end to this need building deep inside him. Before his hormones got completely out of control, there were one or two things he and Jillian had to get straight between them. He wanted her to be honest with him about her feelings, and he wanted her to be honest with herself. He had to let her know that he wouldn't stand in line, not after the bachelors of Jasper Gulch, and certainly not after a ghost. And then he'd show her that he wasn't exactly like her Brian had been. How could he be? Luke Carson was one of a kind.

He took his time removing his hat and letting his foot drop to the porch floor. Unhurriedly straightening his shoulders, he ambled closer.

She'd gone up to the top step, both her hands grasping the railing behind her. He flicked the blade of wild grass he'd been chewing on over the railing, then slowly, surely, reached behind Jillian for her hand.

"Don't ever make me do that again," he whispered.

"Do what?"

Threading her fingers with his own, he drew her up onto the porch, lowering his face to hers at the same time. When his lips were but a hair's breadth away, he said, "Don't ask me to go out with someone else. Do you know why I don't want to go out with anyone else, Jillian?"

She shook her head a fraction of an inch, the movement brushing her lips against his in a featherlight caress that nearly buckled his knees. "Because I only want to be with you."

If he hadn't been so close, he never would have heard the sound echoing deep in her throat. It was erotic, fanciful and so sensual his vision blurred. But it didn't matter, because a second later his lips covered hers, and his eyes closed automatically. He didn't need to see. His other senses took over, flooding him with responses to the softness of her lips beneath his, to the scent of her heated skin and the rustle of her hands as they glided over his shirt and slid around his back.

She fit him so perfectly, her body smooth where his was rough, round where his was flat, soft where his was hard. She was pliant, yet he felt the strength in her slender muscles just below the surface of her skin. Those muscles weren't pushing him away, but straining toward him. It was the headiest thing he'd ever experienced.

In that instant he knew there was nothing in the world more intoxicating than being accepted, wanted, by this woman. It was what he'd been waiting for all his life and why he'd been so impatient and edgy this past year. It was as if everything he'd ever done had led him to this moment in time with this woman. The woman he loved.

There was a time when a realization like that would

have had him breaking out in hives. Now it deepened his breathing and his need.

It made him want more.

The kiss broke, finally, and they both pulled deep breaths to the bottom of their lungs. Jillian tried to straighten, but Luke didn't let her go, angling away only enough to be able to look into her eyes.

"Jillian Daniels, you are some kisser."

It was never easy to think when he turned all that intensity on her, but there was something about the blend of husky desire and that telltale note of teasing in his voice that calmed her in ways she hadn't expected. Hadn't she always known the man had more attitude than he knew what to do with? What she'd never realized was how many responses it brought out in her.

"What am I going to do with you?" she asked.

She could tell what he was thinking by the glint in his eyes. So when he said, "Do you really have to ask?" she was ready with a coy lift of her eyebrows.

Releasing a breath of pent-up air for show, she said, "Yes, I do. I'm still not certain I'm going to stay in Jasper Gulch."

He took a backward step, snagging her hand on his way. "I can deal with honesty. And as long as we're on the subject, I might as well tell you that I intend to change your mind about leaving. But first, I want to make it clear to every bachelor within a hundred-mile radius that you're seeing me."

Jillian couldn't help smiling at his irascible tone. Tilting her head slightly, she said, "And how do you plan to do that?"

"If you agree to have lunch with me at the diner tomorrow, I won't have to do anything. Word will be all over town by the middle of the afternoon, if not sooner. So, will you?"

The blood rushing through her head made it difficult to

make sense of his question. The fact that her emotions were teetering from one extreme to the other didn't help matters, either. But in the end she nodded and said, "Yes, I'll have lunch with you, Luke."

"Good," he declared as if he'd known she'd say yes all along. "Be prepared to answer a million questions."

"Questions?"

"I want to know everything about you."

"Everything?"

"Yup."

"Like what?"

"Like, were did you get your red hair?"

"My hair is not..."

Raising his fingers to her lips to still her denial, he said, "I know, I know. You don't consider your hair red. I think I'm going to like convincing you. But then, there are a lot of things I'm going to like doing with you, learning about you."

"You'll be bored within ten minutes."

The devil-may-care grin he gave her was one of a kind. "I'll be the judge of that."

She couldn't manage honest-to-goodness exasperation, so she gave him a smile. For a moment he went perfectly still, his gaze trained on her mouth. When he came out of his stupor, there was more fire in his eyes.

"The list of things I intend to learn about you is growing longer by the minute, you know."

"That's what worries me."

"I'm not trying to worry you, Jillian. All I want is to get to know you. For starters, you could tell me what you eat for breakfast. And then you could tell me why you decided to become a teacher."

"I eat corn flakes and juice for breakfast. And I became a teacher because of a gray-haired lady who taught English 202. Miss Devine wore orthopedic shoes and bifocals, but she was the only teacher who ever looked deeper than my

worn clothes and shyness. She believed I had the potential
to do anything I set my mind to. And she was right. Now
I'm going to do the same for kids today."

She let the tone of her voice and the angle of her chin
say, "Tell me neither of those tidbits of information are
anything but boring."

Only he didn't look bored. He looked intrigued and interested and so ruggedly handsome he took her breath
away. He placed his hat on his head and went down to the
sidewalk before glancing around at her in a way she was
coming to recognize, the porch light bathing him in yellow
light, casting his eyes in shadow. He wasn't a man prone
to smiles. Maybe that was why the one he gave her that
instant softened her heart more than words could have.

"There's something else I want to know about you, Jillian."

"What's that?"

"When you're ready, I want to hear about Brian."

She looked at him for several seconds without speaking.
She didn't know what to say. She hadn't talked about
Brian in a long, long time, hadn't wanted to or needed to.
What was there to say, except that she'd loved him and
lost him. Talking about him, *thinking* about him, had a
way of making her feel blue, lonely. Sad.

Luke tipped his hat up with one finger, inherent determination evident in the set of his chin, hunger evident in
the light in his eyes. She didn't intend to look deeper, but
once she did, she couldn't look away. There was more than
determination and hunger in the man standing on the sidewalk. There was goodness and honesty and, yes, there was
wistfulness, too.

"Will you tell me about him, Jillian?"

Swallowing the lump in her throat, she nodded. "Yes,
Luke. One of these days, I'd like to do just that."

He grinned his cocky, cowboy, know-it-all grin. And
she answered with one of her own.

"Oh, there's one more thing I plan to do."

"There is?" she asked.

"Yes. I'm going to...better yet, *we're* going to catch that pie thief."

"But why?"

"Because we can't have people in Jasper Gulch stealing food or anything else. It just isn't right."

"But I—"

Rushing in as if she hadn't spoken, he said, "So if you'll prepare something mouth watering and tempting, we'll put it out here and catch this guy once and for all."

"But Luke, I—"

"You are one argumentive woman, do you know that? Trust me on this, Jillian."

"But, Luke, you don't understand. I can't—"

"Sure you can."

The man's sense of honor and duty was obviously every bit as inborn as his stubborn attitude. He simply didn't let a person get a word in edgewise.

"I'm going to be out at Wes Walker's place all morning," he declared. "So I won't see you again until lunch. I'll swing by the office and pick you up."

"But Luke, I—"

He turned on his heel, bounded up the steps and kissed her full on the mouth, only to bound back down again and say, "See you at noon."

Since he was already walking away, Jillian didn't bother answering. She simply stared after him, thinking that he definitely needed to take lessons in listening. But he didn't need any practice perfecting the fine art of kissing. Oh, no, he had that down to an art form. Smiling to herself, she supposed that if he had to be bad at something, she was glad it wasn't kissing.

Oh yes, she was very glad, indeed.

Chapter Eight

For a man who was so good at kissing, Luke was doing an awfully good job of *not* kissing Jillian tonight. Not *quite* kissing her, that is. He'd kissed her on the cheek, on the corner of her mouth, on that sensitive little spot where her eyebrow arched. Every time his lips touched her skin she felt warm all over. It had been a long time since she'd felt warm in exactly this way, a long time since she'd felt so much quiet urgency racing through her.

He'd sauntered into the house at a little before ten, just as he had the first time they'd tried to capture the pie thief. Then, like now, the living room was dark. It was quiet, too, except for his occasional husky whisper and the twangy music playing over the portable radio in the corner. All in all, the scenario for this stakeout was the same as before. Only *she* had changed.

She was still nervous. Why wouldn't she be? The emotions blossoming inside her were scary. They were also as real as the man sitting beside her. That was the wonder of it. Unfortunately, it was also the fear. Since her grandfather hadn't raised a coward, she was doing her best to face her feelings and her fears.

"You mentioned that you went to live with your grandfather when you were twelve. Tell me, Jillian, what did he look like?"

As far as Jillian was concerned, Luke's voice was low, smooth and far from innocent. Just like he was. She waited to answer, her ears straining to pick up the slightest noise from the other side of the open window. Satisfied that nobody was sneaking onto the porch, she finally whispered, "He looked like an ordinary grandpa. He didn't have much hair on top, wore ties on Sundays and sweaters every day of the week."

"No wonder I remind you of him."

She heard the note of sarcasm in Luke's voice, as well as a hint of wry humor. The man was a study in contrasts, and contrarily persistent. And he was wreaking havoc with her senses.

She'd taken a quick shower and donned a pair of crisp, white jeans and a dark purple shirt, then had spent an inordinate amount of time looking through Lisa's recipes. Luke expected her to prepare something to use as bait, preferably something mouth watering. She'd pored over the recipe books, studying each and every entry carefully. Mulligan stew had looked fairly simple to prepare, and she'd almost decided to try her hand at that. But she'd changed her mind because it was simply too hot outside to eat stew, even for a thief.

At the last minute she'd decided to stir up a batch of fudge brownies. Using the oven had heated up the kitchen, but she had to admit the brownies had looked delicious. If she were a thief, she'd be tempted to take them and run herself.

"What was his name?" Luke asked, as if only a few seconds had passed since she'd spoken, instead of a few minutes.

"What was whose name?"

He was sitting next to her on the floor, his arm brushing her shoulder, one leg pulled up, the other stretched out at a comfortable angle. Bringing his face within a few inches of her ear, he whispered, "Your grandfather's, who else?"

Jillian knew exactly what he was up to. The surprising thing was she was enjoying it almost as much as she enjoyed baiting him. "His name was Henry Patrick Finlay."

"I'll bet he had a nickname."

"As a matter of fact, he did."

"Was it Hank?"

She shook her head and smiled.

"Hal?"

She gave her head another shake and him another smile.

"Harry?"

"No."

"Hmm. An Irishman. I'll bet everyone called him Red."

Fighting a smile, she said, "That doesn't prove a thing."

He glided a finger over her cheekbone, across the bridge of her nose and back again. "It proves that I was right, and that you came by your red hair naturally."

Jillian stared up at him through the semidarkness, thinking that he'd been this way all day, haughty one minute, dreamily sensual the next and determined always. True to his word he'd picked her up at his office shortly before noon. He'd tucked her hand into the crook of his elbow and strode into the diner making enough commotion to cause everyone to sit up and take notice, just as he'd intended. Now he seemed just as determined to find out everything about her, past and present.

"What did your grandfather do for a living?"

"He tried his hand at a lot of things, but never made much money at any of them. There was always enough love in that house, but not a lot of anything else. Grandpa had a deep laugh and a story for every occasion. You would have liked him, I'm sure."

Luke didn't know what was going through Jillian's mind, but he recognized the sharp stirrings of desire going through his body. Once again he learned as much about her from what she didn't say as from what she said. Her grandfather had obviously been a poor man. Rather than dwelling on that, she spoke of the love he'd given her.

He was tempted to kiss her, here and now. Good Lord, was he tempted. But the pie thief had gotten away the last time because of one deep, mind-boggling kiss. Luke Carson had a reputation to uphold, but the real reason he didn't kiss her was because he wanted her to feel the same kind of need he was feeling, sense the same degree of attraction, and *want* him as badly as he wanted her. So he didn't kiss her, at least not on the mouth. Instead he leaned closer and whispered a kiss below her ear. If his lips lingered a little longer than he'd intended, he couldn't help it.

"What are you thinking about, Jillian?"

"Oh," she said quietly, her eyelashes fluttering down. "I was just thinking about a psychology class I took in college."

She had to be kidding. He was nuzzling her neck, his desire on the rampage, and she was thinking about a class she took in college?

"Please tell me the class dealt with human sexuality."

"Actually, we studied the type of people that are attracted to certain professions. I set the curve with the paper I wrote concluding that careers in law, journalism and show business draw the most loquacious people. You know, the wordy, talk-a-mile-a-minute types. According to the research I did, other careers such as accounting and veterinary medicine draw a different type of personality entirely."

"Is that so?"

She shook her head. "No, that isn't so. I was completely wrong. You're a veterinarian and you asked me eighteen questions before Melody took our orders for lunch. I've lost track of how many you've asked tonight. If I were to go back and take that class again, I'd have to change my assessment. It seems that veterinary medicine has drawn the most loquacious man on the planet."

"If that's true, then so have you."

Luke's boot creaked, and so did his belt, but the sounds were nothing compared to the deep rasp of his voice, or the way it caused her eyes to drift down and her heart to turn over in her chest. It was true. He did draw her, in so many ways. He drew her laughter and her pique, her curiosity, her interest and her desire. It was strange, but Cori Cassidy, one of Jillian's closest friends, had described her feelings for her soon-to-be husband almost word-for-word.

I wonder what Cori would say if I told her about Luke.

"Who's Cori?"

Jillian hadn't realized she'd spoken out loud—that's how off balance Luke had her emotions. Trying to get back on steady ground, she said, "Cori Cassidy is a friend of mine back in Wisconsin. I met her when she went to live with Ivy Pennington in the house next door to my grandfather's. Cori has a sixteen-year-old daughter who's truly amazing. But then, Cori and Ivy and Travis are pretty amazing, too. Gosh, I can't believe how much I miss all of them. At least I'll be seeing them soon."

Luke didn't move a muscle. That didn't stop the warning drums from pounding inside his head. He didn't get it. Jillian's eyes had drifted shut sensuously mere seconds ago. The next thing he knew, she was talking about how much she missed her friends back in Madison.

"What do you mean you'll be seeing them soon?"

"Didn't I tell you? Cori's getting married the weekend after next. Allison, Lisa and I are going to be bridesmaids in her wedding."

Luke didn't know who the hell Allison was, but he was pretty sure this Cori woman wouldn't be coming all the way to Jasper Gulch to get married. That meant Jillian was going back to Madison even sooner than he'd expected. He didn't like the sound of that one bit. Maybe it was because there were still so many things about her he didn't know. Or maybe it was because the weekend after next was only eleven days away, and that didn't leave him much time to convince her that Jasper Gulch was where she truly belonged.

He considered laying all his cards on the table and blurting out his need for her. But Jillian had needs, too, and he didn't want to make the situation worse.

"Luke, is everything all right?"

"What could possibly be wrong?"

The drums inside his head were getting louder. The strange thing was that they seemed to be accompanied by the soft thud of footsteps and the scrape of a dish sliding across a tabletop.

He turned his head, listening. "Did you hear something?"

His mind cleared, and so did his vision. And then, for the second time in a matter of days, he and Jillian stumbled to their feet and groped their way to the front door. For the second time in a matter of days, they squinted against the sudden brightness of the porch light. And for the second time in a matter of days, the food they'd left on the porch was gone, plate and all.

"I can hardly believe he took my fudge brownies."

Even with everything he had on his mind, Luke heard the amazement in Jillian's voice. It was almost as if she was pleased. He looked at her long and hard, raked his fingers through his hair and decided it was high time he asked her what in tarnation was going on.

"Jillian..."

She emerged from the refrigerator with a pitcher of lemonade in her hand and a query in her eyes. "Can I get you something cold to drink?"

Luke would have preferred a shot of his father's best whiskey, straight up. While he was at it, he wanted to demand to know how long she was planning to be gone. When she was planning to come back. *If* she was planning to come back.

He took the glass from her and downed the contents all at once. Ice cubes jangled as he placed the glass on the counter with a loud thunk. When he looked at Jillian again, he found her watching him over the rim of her glass, and he swore her eyes had never looked so blue, her expression so soft.

"Would you like anything else, Luke?"

Luke knew what he'd like, all right. Replies to a few very important questions. Unfortunately, he didn't trust her answers, and he sure as hell wasn't ready to hear her say that this was just a brief interlude in her life, that she wasn't going to stay here in Jasper Gulch. That she wasn't sure she could ever love again.

He was close enough to hear the soft rustle of her shirt and jeans as she leaned a hip against the counter and crossed her ankles. Something gave way inside him, and raw need took the place of his anger and his trepidation.

"Luke?"

"Hmm?"

"*Would* you like anything else?"

He took the few steps that had separated them and brought his face down to hers. "I'd like this."

He captured her gasp in his own mouth, then gave it back to her in the form of a low moan. He heard her put her glass down. The next thing he knew, her arms were winding around his back, her body curling into his. Another jolt of raw need bucked through him, but he didn't give in to it completely. He'd waited all night to kiss her the way she deserved to be kissed. So, instead of kissing her hard, he placed his hands on either side of her face and opened his mouth over hers.

Her lips were cool and moist, her breath warm and tart, her body soft and pliant and damn near irresistible. He kissed her until he thought he might just go crazy if he couldn't have her. And then he kissed her a little more. His hands finally left her face, only to tangle in her hair, then slowly move lower. Ah, yes, in this moment in time he needed this even more than answers, even more than declarations, even more than whispered endearments and promises of shared tomorrows.

Jillian couldn't think, and yet she knew that this was what she'd been waiting for, this joining of breaths, of heartbeats and of mouths. The realization didn't come from her mind, but from another place deep inside her. She hadn't seen the kiss coming, but once it started there was no turning back. Luke had kissed her before, but this was different. It was at once lusty and infinitely tender, demanding, and quite possibly the most beautiful gift she'd ever received. It was filled with the need of a man for a woman and vice versa—the need to connect on the most basic level and on the highest human plane.

She reveled in the sheer size, strength and heat in the body so close to hers and in the hands on her back. They cupped and kneaded and smoothed over her skin, across her shoulders, down her spine, around her waist. And then, as if in slow motion, they glided up, up, covering her breasts. And she shuddered.

"Oh, Luke."

His answer was unintelligible, spoken so deep in his throat and with so much feeling. But it said more about the need building between them than any well-pronounced oration could have. She wasn't sure why she turned her head toward the front door, but whatever had drawn her attention, drew Luke's, too. She tried to remember if she'd actually heard the scrape of a boot and the clatter of a dish, or if it had been the blood rushing through her veins.

The blur of movement had them untangling their arms and staring at each other for interminable seconds. In the same instant, realization dawned, and they ran to the porch. Luke was the first one there, Jillian two steps behind, both of them staring at the table in disbelief.

"He brought the brownies back."

Jillian nodded. "Yes, it certainly looks that way."

Luke raked a hand through his hair and heaved a great sigh. "I don't get it."

Although it wasn't easy to think with the aftereffects of that kiss so fresh in her mind and on her lips, Jillian resigned herself to the inevitable. She picked up a brownie, raised it to his lips and watched him open his mouth and bite off one corner.

A strange expression crossed his face. His eyes grew large and then narrowed, his lips twisting in a grimace that didn't go away until after he'd reached for a paper napkin and emptied his mouth. He made a sound that probably wasn't in the dictionary, then looked at her in disbelief.

"Not too great, huh?" she asked.

"Did *you* make those?"

"I'm afraid so. That's what I was trying to tell you last night. I can't cook."

"You can't cook."

She shook her head gravely. For a long moment they stood shoulder to shoulder, staring at the pan of innocent-looking brownies. "I can barely boil water. It's hopeless. Just ask Lisa."

At first he appeared too surprised to do more than nod, but gradually his expression changed. With his head tipped back he started to laugh, and so did she. Before they knew how it had happened, they were holding on to each other, their stomachs aching, their chests heaving.

It was a long time before their eyes opened, even longer

before their laughter trailed completely away. When it did, Jillian found herself held tight to Luke's body, his hands around her back, her face turned into the crook of his shoulder. She sighed, pressing a smile-shaped kiss into his neck.

Luke closed his eyes all over again, thinking that everything was right with the world. He and Jillian were going to be fine. Sure, she was going back to Madison in eleven days. That didn't mean she wasn't coming back. A woman couldn't kiss a man the way she'd kissed him earlier and then laugh with him as if there was no one on Earth she'd rather laugh with, unless she cared about him a great deal. Maybe even loved him.

He opened his eyes, wishing he never had to move. For a moment he gazed off into the distance, unseeing. But then a patch of color in the hedge next door caught his eye. His vision cleared, his eyes opening wider.

The hedge moved. The patch of color disappeared. And Luke vaulted over the porch railing, his feet moving before they hit the ground below.

He could hear Jillian calling his name, but he cut through a gap in the hedge without answering. Darting to the left, he skirted the back of the McKenzies' yard and caught the culprit by the scruff of the neck.

"Let go of me, you jerk!"

He hauled the thief—whose mouth showed telltale signs of crumbs—to a stop. There was the rustle of footsteps in the dry grass behind him. And then Jillian called, "Luke, what are you doing to that poor little girl?"

The urchin stopped snarling and fighting, going as still as a fawn trapped in a car's headlights. Luke loosened his hold, but he knew better than to let go completely.

"Do you want to explain?" he asked the thief. "Or shall I?"

The girl tried one last time to shrug Luke's hand from her shoulder, then stuck one hip out, crossed her arms and jutted out her chin defiantly. "What were you trying to do, Uncle Luke? Poison me?"

"Uncle Luke?"

It was Jillian who had spoken, Jillian who was moving forward as if she couldn't believe what she was hearing. Luke scrubbed a hand across his face. With a slow shake of his head and a rumbling sigh, he said, "Jillian, I'd like you to meet your pie thief. This is Haley Fingers Carson. My one and only niece."

"I can't believe Haley could have done such a thing," Clayt said, his voice harsh and raw at the same time. "What am I going to do?" He looked around at the people who were gathered in his living room.

"I don't know, Clayt," Luke muttered. "I just don't know."

"I can't think of anything more effective than a hickory switch behind the woodshed," Cletus said, giving his suspenders a loud snap.

"I can't *spank* her. Maybe she needs counseling."

"Ach," Cletus grumbled. "That girl don't need counseling."

"Maybe you should call Victoria, son," Hugh Carson said gravely.

Shaking his head forlornly, Clayt said, "I can't, Dad. Victoria didn't leave a forwarding address, let alone a telephone number where I could reach her."

"Jumpin' catfish, I wish your mother was here. She'd know what to do. Maybe we should call her."

"You don't need to call Rita in Oregon. I'm tellin' ya, one swift switchin' will cure that child of stealin' once and for all."

"Granddad," Wyatt said, speaking up for the first time, "would you forget about taking a switch to that poor little girl's backside?"

Looking duly chastised and chagrined, Cletus let loose

a loud harrumph and sputtered, "Well, if you don't wanna take my advice, why did you call me over here?"

"We called you to help. And I'm telling you beating that little girl isn't going to help."

"Yeah. I can't believe you'd even suggest such a thing."

"What were you thinking, Granddad?"

"Uh, boys," Hugh said. "I think we're getting a trifle off the track here. Now, what are we going to do about Haley?"

If the situation hadn't been so serious, Jillian would have smiled at the way the men took turns looking at each other and shaking their heads. Clayt and his father had taken to wringing their hands; Luke was kneading the back of his neck; Sheriff McCully shifted from one foot to the other; and at this rate, Cletus would wear out a perfectly good pair of suspenders by the end of the night. All the men had raked their fingers through hair that bore a slight indentation where a cowboy hat had sat most of the day. Unfortunately, none of them had been able to come up with what they considered a solution to Haley's problems or just punishment for what she'd done.

It was pretty obvious that none of the men in the room had the faintest idea what to do with one rebellious little girl. It was just as obvious that each and every one of them loved the child more than they could say. Jillian had been there when Luke had delivered his niece to her father, and she'd seen Clayt's look of disbelief slowly turn into worry, disappointment and finally a fledgling kind of belief that he could handle this situation if he really tried. Surely, Jillian thought to herself, a child who was surrounded by so much love would be all right.

"Why don't you bring Haley in, son?"

"Yeah," Luke agreed. "Maybe she'll be able to tell us why she did it."

Looking for all the world like a man who would rather

stare down a charging bull than punish his little girl, Clayt
scrubbed a hand across his bleary eyes, then slowly turned
on his heel to do as his father suggested. He was back
seconds later, his hand resting stiffly on his daughter's
shoulder.

Haley was wearing bright pink jeans that had a tear in
one knee and a flowered shirt that had probably been clean
when she put it on. Her brown hair was sticking out in
every direction, the freckles across her nose more evident
than usual on her pale face.

"Haley?" Clayt asked. "Do you have anything to say
for yourself?"

Staring at her shoes, the child slunk to the couch without
a word.

"Can you at least tell me *why* you stole Jillian's food?"

Still the child said nothing.

Jillian glanced around the room, then quietly strode to
the sofa where Haley was sitting. Going down on her
haunches, she kept her voice as low as possible and asked,
"Haley? Are you sorry for taking the food off Lisa's
porch?"

"Guess so. 'Specially those brownies." She stuck her
tongue out for emphasis.

The men let loose barks of laughter, then clamped their
mouths shut as if they suddenly realized this wasn't the
time or the place.

Smiling wryly, Jillian said, "I can't cook worth beans,
can I?"

The child's head came up, her eyes wide, her mouth
slightly open. "You can't?"

Jillian shook her head, and in a voice smaller than she
was, Haley said, "It's okay, I can't, either. My mama's
gonna teach me."

"Ya see? I told you that child needs a mother!"

There was a slight scuffle behind her, followed by a little

yelp from Cletus. Ignoring everyone else, Jillian said, "Do you know what I think, Haley?"

The child looked at her skeptically for a long time, her eyes narrowed, her expression calculating. "What?"

"I don't think you did this to be mean."

"I'm a Carson, but I ain't mean. Aren't mean. Isn't mean. Anyway, I didn't wanna do anything wrong. It's boring out here. There's nobody to play with. So I rode my new bike to town. Hiding in the hedge next to your house was fun. You and that other pretty lady do stuff nobody else does, like eating late at night and laughing. I like watching you. And then I got hungry."

Her voice trailed away as if she'd said more than she'd intended. Jillian heard a little scuffle behind her. The next thing she knew, Clayt stepped into her field of vision, albeit jerkily, making her wonder if someone had given him a little shove.

"I think you have something to say to Jillian, Haley," he insisted.

Her gaze flew to the toe of her shoe all over again, but this time she said, "I'm sorry, ma'am."

"Apology accepted. But there's one more thing I need from you."

"There is?"

Nodding, Jillian said, "Do you still have that yellow dish you took last week?"

At Haley's slow nod, she said, "That dish was a gift from a dear friend of mine, and I'd like it back. Would you go get it, please?"

The child was off the couch in a flash, across the room in a flurry and up the stairs before anyone could bat an eye. She was back again minutes later, Ivy's antique dish in one hand, one of Lisa's mismatched plates in the other.

Luke couldn't believe his eyes. Haley was walking toward Jillian, her head held high, her eyes glowing with admiration. The same nine-year-old girl who had won a spitting contest last week and could hold her own with any boy in town had turned into a princess in the blink of an eye. What's more, she seemed genuinely sorry for what she'd done.

All because of Jillian. The woman was amazing. He'd always suspected that she'd make a wonderful teacher, but now he realized she was going to make an even better mother. Kids had always figured into Luke's future. The hazy, shadowy forms of boys and girls had loomed somewhere on the horizon. Suddenly the horizon was staring him in the face.

He recognized the need pooling low in his body. What red-blooded, able-bodied man wouldn't? But until that instant, he'd never realized just what that need entailed. This was more than lust for a woman. What he was feeling was so much greater, so much stronger than anything he'd ever experienced before. Somehow the children he wanted were no longer vague, nondescript creatures. They were Jillian's children and his, redheaded waifs or brown-haired hellions. It didn't matter which, as long as they were theirs.

Jillian chose that instant to look up at him, and if he lived to be a hundred, he'd never forget the way she looked at that moment, her hair mussed, her white jeans dirty, her eyes artfully serene. The smile she gave him went straight to his heart. He wondered what he would do if he couldn't convince her that they both wanted the same thing.

That old coot Cletus claimed her attention, drawing her into a conversation about people she didn't even know. Soon Jillian was laughing, and so was everyone else in the room. All except Luke, that is.

Deciding that if he couldn't beat them, he might as well join them, he strode to her side and reached for her hand. Wyatt and Clayt nudged each other, and Cletus guffawed to beat the band. Luke didn't care. He had eleven days to convince Jillian that what she really wanted and needed was him. He may have had his work cut out for him, but that didn't matter. He had eleven days, and he intended to make the most of each and every one.

"Come on," he whispered, close to her ear, "there's a view out over the plains you can't miss."

She said goodbye to everyone, including Haley, then turned to him as if she sensed that he had something important on his mind. After taking her hand, he pushed through the same door he'd been walking through all his life. For some reason, this time felt different.

Clayt's best cattle dog, General Custer, raised his head when they passed, but except for the dry grass crinkling beneath their shoes, and crickets chirruping farther away, the night was quiet. He felt Jillian's eyes on him when they reached the corral. Staring straight ahead, he said, "Look at that sky. There still isn't a cloud in sight."

"Is that what you brought me out here to talk about, Luke? The sky and the clouds and the drought?"

He rested his forearms along the top of the gate and hiked one boot onto the lowest rung. In a voice nearly as quiet as the wind, he said, "Actually, I was thinking that this would be the perfect time and the perfect place to tell me about Brian."

Chapter Nine

Luke saw the indecision in Jillian's eyes, and for a moment he saw the pain. He wasn't at all certain she was going to do as he'd asked and finally tell him about Brian. She glanced away from him, her gaze on something far in the distance. After a time she began to speak.

"I met Brian Kincaid during a snowstorm the winter I turned twenty-one. He was everything I wasn't—confident, popular, funny. Neither of us had two nickels to our name, but we were both going to be somebody. I was going to be a teacher, and he was going to be a medivac pilot, flying to medical emergency centers all over the country.

"Brian loved to fly, and he loved to take chances. It was the only thing we ever argued about. But I couldn't have changed that part of him any more than I could have changed his love of the sky. When I passed my first final exam and he got his first job flying for a small airfreight company, we knew it was only a matter of time before we had everything we dreamed of. My parents were gone, and he and his father didn't get along, but that was okay because we had each other."

A cow lowed in the distance; an owl hooted. And Jillian talked on. Luke listened to every word she said, the soft, clear tone of her voice drawing him into the story of her past like the tender brush of fingertips and the coolness of deep shade. He could practically see Brian Kincaid in his mind, from his laughing brown eyes to his second-hand flight coveralls. Her words made it easy to picture wild flowers in soda bottles, and two young people falling in love.

It was beautiful. It left a bad taste in Luke's mouth, a bad feeling in the pit of his stomach. He'd wanted her to tell him about Brian. Now he almost wished he'd passed. Jillian had loved someone. Someone other than him. Someone who sounded pretty darned incredible. Hell, for all Luke knew, she might love him still.

He'd never much cared for standing in line, and he was hard-pressed to know what to do about it this time. Before he could figure it all out, there was one more thing he had to ask. "How did Brian die, Jillian?"

Her voice, when it came, was quieter, throatier, as she told him about Brian's medical airplane going down during a snowstorm in the mountains. And though she didn't say it, Luke could picture a young woman with long red hair waiting for word a thousand miles away. Brian Kincaid had been twenty-five.

Neither of them spoke when she was through with the telling. There didn't seem to be anything to say. So he did the only thing he could. He kissed her full on the mouth with all the intensity and urgency that was bottled up inside him. His chest heaved, but he didn't break the kiss. He just wrapped his arms around her and pulled her hard against him. He couldn't disguise his body's reaction, and he didn't want to. This was what he wanted, needed to do. When the kiss finally ended, they were both winded, but at least there was no doubt in either of their minds that they were both very much alive.

He took her home a short time later. They talked on the way, about inconsequential things mostly. And he kissed her at the door all over again. But when he pulled away from the curb in front of her house, he was painfully aware that it was well after midnight. And that he now had only ten days to move to the front of that invisible line and convince her to stay.

"Clayt didn't really ground Haley for the rest of her life, did he?" Jillian asked.

Luke made a soothing sound to the mare who'd gotten a little too friendly with a barbed wire fence, then slowly, carefully, pulled another stitch tight. "Clayt threatened to, but he was just blowing off steam. He knows that's a little too harsh for a nine-year-old. I feel sorry for him. He can't go anywhere without running into somebody all too willing to offer him advice. But at least now he knows why Haley was never hungry and wanted to sleep until noon."

"Like they say, knowing is half the battle, right?"

Luke shrugged, thinking that the man who'd made that statement couldn't have heard the depth of feeling in the voice of the woman *he* loved, when she was talking about another man. There probably wasn't a saying in any language befitting that, unless you counted *Oh, hell.*

"You're awfully quiet tonight."

Glancing over his right shoulder where Jillian was perched on one of the corral fences on the Carson ranch, he figured he had good reason to be quiet. Three more days had passed. It still hadn't rained, and Jillian still hadn't told him how she felt about him. What was worse, there didn't seem to be a darn thing he could do about either one of those things.

"Do horses out here make a habit of getting too friendly with barbed wire fences?" she asked.

"I suppose it goes with the territory."

"Do all the animals you doctor stand there so obediently?"

"If they know what's good for them, they do."

Jillian couldn't help smiling at Luke's cocksure attitude, but she saw through it tonight, all the way to the heart of a very special man. Luke Carson was no saint, and he was no stranger to swearing, but he cared about the animals out here. That mare wasn't afraid of him. In fact, she seemed immensely relieved to be placing herself in Luke's capable hands.

Jillian watched in silence while he put the finishing touches on the horse's injuries, then waited as he slowly climbed to the top of the fence beside her. After the horse trotted off to the other side of the corral, Luke heaved a weary sigh. From the corner of her eye, she saw him knock the dust from his hat, then slowly place it on his head.

She and Luke seemed to be the only people around tonight. Clayt had taken Haley to a movie in Pierre, and evidently Hugh was playing poker with Cletus and his cronies down at the Crazy Horse. The sun was gone in the west, but the glowing hues of peach, coral and rose still swirled together in the sky. Making idle conversation, she asked, "How many times would you say you've sat on a fence and looked at those same hills?"

She turned her head so she could see the clear-cut lines in Luke's profile. He shrugged again and moved a blade of prairie grass to the other side of his mouth. "More times than I can count, that's for sure. My father always says there's something in those rolling plains that instills quiet in the hearts of most men."

Trying to pinpoint exactly what the edge in his voice meant, she said, "Not in yours?"

He looked a little surprised that she'd picked up on that, but he answered her after a time. "They don't instill quiet in me in exactly the way they do in my father and Clayt. Ranching is in their blood. It's not in mine. Even as a kid

I had a hard time sitting around waiting for it to rain, waiting for the corn and hay to grow.''

Jillian still didn't know what he was trying to say, or why his voice sounded so weary. Although she was pretty sure he wasn't even aware of it, he'd slid to his feet on the ground as if he couldn't sit still. Hooking his fingers through his belt loops, he leaned against the fence and crossed his ankles.

''I had to put four steers down at Ben Jacobs's place today.''

Suddenly she understood. No wonder he was quiet. No wonder he was weary. No wonder he didn't feel like sitting still. People out here weren't rich, and this winter was going to be leaner than usual. Ranchers sold cattle for cash then turned around and used that cash to feed their families. Ben Jacobs would undoubtedly feel the pinch when there were four less head of cattle to go around come winter.

Those steers must have been very sick. Even so, it couldn't have been an easy thing for Luke to do. No matter what he said about those rolling plains in the distance instilling quiet in the hearts of men, he cared about these people, and he hurt when they hurt.

''Have you ever thought about leaving Jasper Gulch, Luke?''

''And miss out on all this grandeur?''

His voice was losing its steely edge. And she was glad. At least she could do that much for him.

He turned in her direction. Hooking one arm over the top of the fence, he said, ''I went away to college. Except for a couple of summers when I came home, I was gone for seven years. I made a lot of friends at Michigan State University, but there was never any question that I'd come back here.''

She smiled and said, ''What I want to know is how on

earth so many women could have left town when they knew you were coming back.''

His head came up like lightning, his eyes going straight to hers. "Does that mean you think I'd be worth sticking around for?''

Jillian didn't know what to say. She'd meant her query to be teasing. Wasn't it just like Luke to take her seriously? She knew exactly what he was asking. After all, the man could move without making a sound, but when he wanted to make a point, he was about as subtle as a herd of elephants. He wanted to know if she'd stay if he asked, and if she was planning to make Jasper Gulch her home.

How could she answer him when she didn't even know the answer herself? Hoping to ease the sting of her silence, she said, "If you're fishing for compliments, Luke, it isn't necessary. You must know I think you're very special.''

Luke was a swearing man. But not one curse came to mind. He'd never felt so frustrated in his life. Not when he was trying to decide what to be when he grew up, not when he'd first realized that girls were different from boys but was too young to do anything about it. Not even when he'd faced the fact that the town of Jasper Gulch was going to die if its remaining citizens didn't do something to save it. This frustration was different, because he couldn't shake the feeling that when it came to Jillian, time was running out.

"Are you ready to go?'' she asked, drawing him from his dark thoughts.

He glanced at the last remaining color in the sky and nodded. They walked side by side to his dusty truck. He helped her up, then strode around to the driver's side. Neither of them said much during the two-mile drive back to Elm Street, but one thought played through his mind the entire time.

Another day was over. And there were only eight left.

* * *

Luke stepped onto the sidewalk in front of the Jasper Gulch Animal Clinic and stopped. A small group of spectators had gathered near the library steps across the street, and Isabell Pruitt was at the front. Seeing old Isabell with her Ladies Aid Society hens wasn't anything new, but seeing her smiling sure was.

A few of the ladies were talking quietly, but most of them were watching and listening to the story being read on the library steps. He did a quick head count and came up with nine children of various ages sitting on the steps, looking up with rapt attention. And in the center of them all sat Jillian.

The sun glinted off the hard cover of the book in her hands, her voice holding the children spellbound. Turning the page so everyone could see the picture, she said, "How many of you would like to live in a castle like this? Hold up your right hand."

Eight right hands shot into the air and one left hand.

Isabell Pruitt started forward. Before she'd made it two steps, Jillian's voice rang with calm acceptance and throaty laughter. "Hold up your other right hand, Billy. That's it."

The children didn't seem to notice anything out of the ordinary, but all the adults had witnessed Jillian's unique ability to correct a child without damaging his self-esteem.

Jillian leaned forward, a sunbeam delineating the smooth line of her jaw and the creamy expanse of the side of her neck. A bolt of sexual attraction came out of nowhere with so much force it nearly knocked Luke's feet out from under him. With the attraction came something else that was even more powerful. He *wanted* Jillian Daniels, in his bed, in his life, at his side. She stirred his longings, but seeing the way she was with those children stirred his paternal urges all over again.

There wasn't a child alive who wouldn't benefit from being in her classroom. Jillian was going to make a wonderful teacher, there was no doubt about it. But Luke had his doubts as to where her classroom was going to be located. She was leaving tomorrow, and he didn't know if she was coming back.

The breeze picked up a lock of hair that had escaped the clasp at her nape, blowing the wispy tresses across her face. Automatically smoothing them away, she chose that moment to look his way, her gaze meeting his from the other side of the street. She said something to Haley, and a moment later his niece waved wholeheartedly. Jillian smiled, and Luke felt as if the wind had been knocked out of him. He returned Haley's wave and did his best to return Jillian's grin. But it wasn't easy to smile, when what he wanted to do was sprint across the street and kiss her in front of Isabell, God and everybody else.

Jillian passed the book around, allowing the children to take a moment to study the beautiful illustrations. She was aware of the children's exclamations, and of some of the adults' praises, too. But her attention was trained on the man standing on the other side of the street.

Luke's feet were planted on the concrete, his stance wide, his hands resting lightly on his hips. She couldn't see his expression, yet she felt the intensity of his gaze all the way from here. In that instant she knew why she'd tried so hard to steer clear of him when she first came to Jasper Gulch. It was because he made her feel. And that felt very dangerous. It would have been safer not to feel anything, but she'd decided a long time ago that she couldn't, wouldn't, go through her life numb on the inside. Caring people made life worth living. After Brian died, the caring people in her life had consisted of a handful of very special friends. It was true that they were mostly women, but even her male friends had never made her heart race or her thoughts turn warm, her body languid and wanting.

Only Luke did that.

She knew he loved her. He hadn't come out and said it, but it was there in the way he watched her, in the way he touched her, in the way he wanted her but didn't take her. He loved her, and he was waiting for her to love him in return.

Jillian knew in her heart that she cared for him a great deal. For some reason she couldn't bring herself to say those three little words. Something was holding her back. Whatever it was, it was also drawing her to Madison.

She was leaving tomorrow. And it felt like the hardest thing she'd ever done.

Last night Luke had come right out and asked her if she was coming back. She couldn't answer. In all honesty, she didn't know. She wasn't sure if she was strong enough to come back, strong enough to let go of the last remnants of the protection she had around her heart. If she came back, she'd have to face the fact that she might love him. If she did that, she'd have to face the fact that she could lose him. And she just didn't know if she could live through such a loss again.

Haley handed the book back to her. Plastering a smile on her face once again, Jillian began to read the story about castles and magic and characters who lived happily ever after.

"I think that's everything," Lisa said, dropping her suitcase into the trunk next to Jillian's.

Glancing at the dark windows behind her, Jillian said, "Do you have your extra set of keys?"

"Yes."

"Your sunglasses?"

"Mmm-hmm."

"Maps?"

"Yup."

"What about the Western-style bikini with the fringe on it for Cori and that horrible spandex swimsuit with the horseshoes for Travis? I can't imagine where you found such skimpy swimwear—with a Western theme no less—

but I'm still not sure you should give it to Cori and Travis as a wedding gift, Lisa.''

Lisa's dark eyes lit up despite the fact that it was only 4:00 a.m. ''Travis and Cori are taking a cruise for their honeymoon. Trust me. They'll love the gifts. And yes, they're in my big suitcase.''

Jillian did a mental check of the bags and cases in the trunk, then strode to the side of the car where she peered into the open windows. Her purse was already on the floor in the front, and the cooler containing sandwiches and sodas was in the back. ''It looks as if we have everything, Lisa, and yet it feels like I'm forgetting something.''

Lisa closed the trunk as quietly as possible. She waited to speak until after she strode to the door on the driver's side of the car. Meeting Jillian's gaze over the top, she finally asked, ''Did you say goodbye to Luke?''

There was no sense wondering how Lisa could have known the reason for Jillian's unease. Before she could admit it or deny it, a silver truck turned the corner and slowly pulled to a stop at the curb. The engine was cut, the door opened, and a pair of scuffed brown cowboy boots were planted on the hard ground.

Lisa whistled under her breath, but all Jillian could do was stare at Luke. He had the look of a man begging for trouble. She wasn't sure if he'd left his Stetson in the truck or at home, but his hair looked a shade or two darker than usual, making her wonder if he'd just stepped out of the shower.

They squared off opposite each other across the narrow front yard, not speaking, not moving, barely breathing. Swallowing the nerves that seemed to have climbed to her throat, Jillian tried to think of some way to break the tension of the moment. She let her gaze stray to the front of his truck, then back to him. With a small lift of her eyebrows, she called, ''Your lights are on.''

He started. Reaching inside the open window, he cut the

lights and said, "It seems to be becoming a habit of mine."

He took a few steps toward her, then stopped abruptly when he realized that they weren't alone. Casting both of them a long, knowing look, Lisa faked an offhand shrug and said, "Maybe I'd better make sure I turned off the stove. And the lights. And I'd better double-check the windows, too. In case it rains and all."

When Jillian and Luke still didn't move or answer, she flipped her hair behind her shoulders and added, "Yup, that's just what I'll do. No need for either of you to help. I've got it covered. I'll just go on inside. Shouldn't take me more than, say, ten minutes or so."

Neither Luke nor Jillian glanced her way. She didn't say another word, the quiet snap of the screen door the only indication that she'd gone inside.

"She's subtle," Luke said.

"About as subtle as an earthquake."

He smiled. And so did Jillian.

Suddenly neither of them seemed to know where to look. Luke glanced down, Jillian to the side. Within seconds their gazes collided all over again.

"This is awkward," she whispered.

"I didn't intend it to be."

"I know."

"You're getting an early start," he said.

"It's a nine-hour drive to Madison on a good day, plus the air-conditioning went out in Lisa's car, and we'd like to get as far as possible before the temperature gets too unbearable."

"I see."

Their gazes met, held.

"Did you really think I could let you leave without saying goodbye, Jillian?"

She watched his lips move over the words, the sound

of his voice as dusky as secrets whispered in the dark of night. Of course, it *was* still the dark of night.

"I wouldn't have blamed you if you had."

Shrugging, he asked, "The wedding is tomorrow?"

Jillian nodded. "It starts at four o'clock. I talked to Ivy and Allison last night. The place sounded like a madhouse. But knowing them, by tomorrow everything will be running as smooth as glass. The ceremony will take place out in the gardens. Allison will probably cry. Cori is her mother, after all. Ivy will, too, because that's the way Ivy is. And then Lisa will make some outrageous toast at the garden reception. And everyone will laugh."

"I'm going to miss you, you know."

Luke saw Jillian's eyelashes flutter down and knew he probably shouldn't have said that, even though it was the truth. Hell, he probably shouldn't have even come. All he'd done was postpone the inevitable. She was still going to leave. Sure, maybe it had given him another ten minutes with her, a chance to appreciate the way her black tank top hugged her breasts and the way her tan shorts smoothed over her hips and thighs, but in the end she would still...

"I'll miss you, too, Luke."

...get in that car and head back to Madison where she grew up, where all her friends were waiting, where she was one interview away from obtaining a teaching position...

What did she say?

He glanced at her sharply. And he knew he'd heard right. She really *was* going to miss him. His chest expanded. Hot damn. He'd made a wise choice when he'd decided to come. He'd known it all along.

Lisa came out of the house. Stopping on the top step, she said, "Should I go back inside and make sure the toilet isn't running or something?"

Luke and Jillian both shook their heads, both laughed.

"Nah," Luke answered. "You'd probably better get going if you want to get there in time for some of Ivy's famous fidget pie."

He wasn't expecting the soft brush of fingertips on his arm, or Jillian's gentle reach on tiptoe to place a goodbye kiss on his mouth. He wasn't expecting it, but he drank it up like a man too long denied.

It was over within seconds and didn't tell him if she was coming back or staying. Luke knew he was in for the longest weekend of his life.

He reached for her hand and held it, holding her gaze at the same time. This close, he could see her fatigue, her indecision. He knew she could see the red lines in his own eyes and the squint marks next to them that seemed to have gotten deeper these past few weeks. But he hoped that if she looked long enough, she'd see the truth, too. That here was where she wanted to be. Here was where she belonged. Here. With him.

Lowering her gaze, she turned toward the car. He held her door while she climbed in, closed it with a quiet click. He took a step back when Lisa started the engine. "Drive carefully," he called to her. "And give the bride and groom my best."

"I will. Keep an eye on the store for me."

To Jillian he said, "Catch the bouquet."

The car inched backward in the driveway. It was still dark out, but he could see Jillian clearly through her open window. Her gaze was fixed on him.

She didn't answer. Or smile. She waited until they were on the street, and then she waved.

Chapter Ten

Luke pulled his truck into one of the last available parking spaces on Main Street and cut the engine. The downtown section of the village of Jasper Gulch was normally as deserted as it could get at six o'clock on a Saturday night. The store owners had all closed up shop a couple of hours ago, and the Crazy Horse crowd didn't usually get revved up until after dark. But tonight the street was lined with dusty pickup trucks and cars, because DoraLee had brought in a mechanical bull just like she did every year right before Rodeo Days began.

Luke had spent most of the day in a saddle, helping Clayt and their father round up the cattle that had gotten it into their heads to break down a section of fence near the back of the property and run hell-bent in no particular direction. Those cattle had to have been the orneriest, rangiest, most stubborn animals in the entire state of South Dakota. Long before they'd gotten them corralled, the Carson men's tempers had surpassed anything the cattle could dish out.

Or course, Luke, Clayt and Hugh Carson blamed it on

the drought. That was easier to talk about than the woman problems they were all having. Clayt was worried sick about Haley; and Hugh claimed he didn't understand his wife any better now than he had the day he married her thirty-seven years ago. When push came to shove, the silver-haired Carson admitted that he missed the boys' mother, and there wasn't much he wouldn't do to have her come home.

Throwing up his hands, he'd said, "I've tried every way I know to bring that woman back here where she belongs. I've sputtered and badgered and ignored her. I knew she was trouble the day she placed her hands on her hips and informed me that all the sweet talk in the world wouldn't land her in the sack with me until I put a ring on her finger."

Leaning back in their saddles, Clayt and Luke had both grimaced a little at the thought of their mother in that context. Looking out at the hills dotted with cattle that were getting more rangy every day as they searched for the rich green grass that used to be growing right under their hooves, the brothers had remained silent. They didn't have much to offer their father in the way of advice. It seemed that none of the Carsons had much luck when it came to keeping a woman down on the farm.

Eventually, they'd gotten the cattle corralled and the fences mended. Hugh and Clayt had both invited Luke in for a thick steak and a cold beer, but he'd declined. He'd gone home where he'd scrubbed the day's sweat and grime from his skin in a lukewarm shower, then donned a clean pair of jeans and a shirt that wasn't too wrinkled, intent upon heading to the diner for the Saturday-night special. He figured that had to be better than moping around his place or his dad's or brother's, waiting for Monday to roll around again.

He opened his door and stepped to the ground just like he had a thousand times before. His wince was brand-new.

He supposed it could have been the result of a sore muscle—one of the aftereffects of being tossed on his rear end by his own danged horse earlier that afternoon. But Luke knew better. This wince came from worry, plain and simple. It had a name, too. Unrequited love.

He started toward the diner, taking in the faded awnings and weathered siding. On the other side of the writing on the window he could see Isabell Pruitt and Opal Graham taking turns nodding and wagging their tongues.

It was a good thing nobody was behind him, because he turned on his heel so suddenly anybody following would have run into him for sure. Not that he would have cared. Luke Carson was simply in no mood to deal with Isabell Pruitt tonight.

An old Kenny Rogers tune was playing on the jukebox when he pushed through the Crazy Horse's door. Good old "Lucille." Eyeing the dim, hazy room, he figured the song was fitting, somehow, and so was the saloon's nondescript interior.

DoraLee winked from the other side of the bar, and a couple of the die-hard regulars held up their beers in salutation. Boomer Brown and a bunch of the other bachelors were gathered around the mechanical bull. Luke nodded to them all, then strode to the back of the room where a light-haired man was staring into his beer.

Wyatt didn't look up when Luke approached. He didn't haul his big feet out of the way so Luke could take a seat at the other side of the table, either. He just tightened his long-fingered grip on the long-necked bottle of beer in front of him and said, "I didn't think it was possible."

Luke accepted the cold bottle from DoraLee and took a couple of good swigs before lowering it to the table and studying the man who had been his best friend for over thirty years. Wyatt was normally the most even-tempered man in town. The fact that he was in a foul mood tonight was just one more thing that seemed fitting, somehow.

"What didn't you think was possible?"

"I didn't think the awning over my sister's diner could have faded any more. I didn't think the buildings lining Main Street could have dulled any more than they had. And it isn't just the drought, no matter what anybody says. It's as if Lisa and Jillian took all the color with them when they left town yesterday morning."

Luke regarded his friend with somber curiosity. After taking another long slug of beer, he said, "At least you know Lisa's coming back."

"A lot of good it does me when she won't give me the time of day."

Now that Luke thought about it, Wyatt had spent a lot of time staring after Jillian's dark-haired friend. Lisa Markman didn't strike Luke as the uppity type. She'd made no bones or excuses about the fact that she'd come to Jasper Gulch to find a husband. She'd gone out with more than a dozen of the area bachelors already. Luke wasn't counting, but the rest of the men sure were.

Aware of the cold dent the beer made in his empty stomach, Luke reached for a handful of nuts and said, "As far as I know, Wyatt, she hasn't turned anyone down the first time he's asked."

"Yeah, I know. She had dinner with you."

"I explained how that came about. You know nothing happened."

Wyatt slid his fingers up and down the neck of the bottle in front of him. "Lucky for you it didn't. I could have lost my badge. I still might, if Boomer doesn't stop bragging about what happened the night he took her out. She even went out with that mama's boy Grover Andrews."

"She hasn't gone out a second time with either of them."

"I suppose that's some consolation."

"So why don't you ask her?" Luke asked levelly.

"Why? She crosses the street to avoid meeting me face-to-face. She hides behind her menu to keep from looking at me in the diner. Shoot. She might as well wear a sign around her neck that flashes Stop whenever I come near."

"Any idea why?"

"Not a clue. But I intend to find out when she gets back."

A few silent-filled minutes later, the door opened, and a hot breeze snuck in along with Jason Tucker. Wyatt raised his beer to Luke, and since there didn't seem to be much else to say, they both said the only thing they could think of.

"Damn drought, anyway."

Cletus pulled up a chair, and so did Jason and Boomer. Luke and Wyatt stared at their beer bottles while talk swirled around them.

"Heard one of the farriers got kicked in the head this morning," Boomer declared.

"I heard it took old Doc Masey twenty minutes and eighteen stitches to sew his forehead back together."

"The drought's making the animals unpredictable. There ain't no doubt about it."

"We need rain."

"We need it soon."

Eyeing Luke, Cletus asked, "Has the governor called you back, boy?"

Luke nodded. "Yesterday afternoon. Some reporter from one of the news stations in Sioux Falls got wind of our campaign to have water trucked into the area. Between that and our ad luring women to Jasper Gulch, they want to feature us on the six o'clock news."

DoraLee set a round of beers in the center of the table. Giving Luke a broad wink, she said, "Nice going, Luke. And nice haircut."

Luke accepted the ribbing he took from Jason about wanting to look his best on national television. But truth be told, he hadn't made a special trip into Ed's Barbershop because he gave a rip what the rest of America thought about the way he looked. He'd done it because there was still a chance that Jillian might come back to Jasper Gulch. And he figured a fella couldn't be too prepared.

Clayt ambled in a short time later. A short time after that, someone put more quarters in the jukebox. Luke noticed when one of the new women in town dragged Clayt onto the dance floor. He noticed the way Mel's eyes were spewing daggers, too. And damned if it didn't look as if that loudmouth Boomer was cozying up to DoraLee.

Tracy Gentry, who bagged groceries for her grandparents in the town's only grocery store, tried to talk to Luke. He admitted that he felt a little sorry about the fact that she'd gotten her ear hairs singed for her trouble. But he couldn't help it. There was only one woman he wanted to talk to. There was only one woman he wanted, period.

And she'd danged well better try to catch that blasted bouquet.

Jillian breathed in the fragrant air and followed the curving flagstone walkway to the back of the English garden. Cori's cottage peeked through the gaps in the lilac hedge surrounding it on three sides, and everywhere flowers bloomed in a gorgeous array of color. The wedding had been perfect, just as she'd known it would be. Jillian had never seen a more beautiful bride than Cori in her long white dress and the delicate wreath of baby's breath and yellow roses encircling her blond hair. Or maybe what made Cori appear so ethereally beautiful was the way Travis, her new husband, looked at her.

If Jillian closed her eyes, she could picture Cori the way she'd been the first time she'd seen her—sixteen, pregnant and scared. She wasn't scared anymore, and she certainly wasn't pregnant, although she and Travis were talking about adding to the family as soon as possible. Allison was sixteen, now, and chose that instant to look at Jillian across the garden. The girl smiled and waved, and Jillian's heart swelled.

She'd been gone less than a month, yet she was amazed at how different everything seemed. The pale yellow house with its creamy painted porches and light blue shutters looked more like a picture in a fairy tale than she remembered. What's more, the house was literally surrounded with flowers in every color of the rainbow. Fat clouds dotted the sky, and the barest breeze stirred air that was heavy with humidity.

Jillian could see the rooftop dappled with shade of the house next door, where she'd lived with her grandfather. She'd walked this same path to Cori's cottage countless times, had hurried through Ivy's kitchen door so often it had long since become second nature. Why, then, did she have the feeling that everything had changed?

Ivy's Garden, the bed and breakfast inn Ivy and Cori ran together, looked as if it could have been lifted from the glossy pages of a magazine. Women in gauzy dresses floated over freshly mown grass while men in suits and ties stood in dark contrast to the pastel colors of late summer. Butterflies flitted from one flower garden to the next. Arbors were heavy with roses, and birds were singing high in the maple tree in the side yard. Brian had kissed her for the first time underneath that maple tree.

And yet it wasn't Brian she was missing.

"Jillian?"

Crossing her hands over her heart, she turned in a half circle and found Cori hurrying toward her, her long gown floating behind her like a cloud. "You've been awfully quiet since you got back."

"I was just reacquainting myself with your gardens."

"And?" Cori asked, her eyes knowing, her smile soft and serene.

"Everything is so lush and green here. In comparison, the colors in Jasper Gulch are weathered, faded. And yet

I don't think I've ever felt more alive in any other place in my life."

"Maybe it isn't the place that makes you feel alive."

Jillian didn't know how Cori had become so smart, but what she'd said was true. Jillian *did* feel more alive in Jasper Gulch, and it had little to do with geography. An hour ago she'd caught a glimpse of a man wearing a black cowboy hat. It had turned out to be one of the carpenters on Travis's construction crew, but before she'd realized that it wasn't Luke, her breath had caught in her throat and she was already smiling in anticipation.

"I'm going to miss you."

Cori's soft, clear voice drew Jillian from her thoughts. There was no sense wondering how Cori could have known that Jillian was going back to Jasper Gulch, when Jillian had only just now realized it herself. Enjoying the moment of closeness with her friend, she smiled and said, "Luke said the same thing before I left Jasper Gulch."

"What else did he say when you left?"

Shaking her head at her memories, Jillian said, "He told me to catch the bouquet."

Cori laughed, but before either of them could say any more, Lisa emerged from the other side of the rose arbor, her pale yellow bridesmaid's dress an exact replica of Jillian's and Allison's.

"Oh, Jillian, there you are!" she exclaimed.

"I should have known I'd find the three of you here," Ivy declared, breathlessly tucking a strand of gray hair into the bun at the back of her head. "It's where you always went when you wanted to talk about boys."

"Mom?" Allison called. "Can Heather and I try to catch the bouquet?"

"If you promise to wait ten years to get married."

"Twenty," Travis corrected, striding to his new wife's side.

"Don't worry about it, Travis. I'm the one who's going to catch that bouquet," Lisa declared.

"Not if my sister, Rachel, has anything to say about it."

"Cori's throwing it to me."

"Mom will toss it fair and square, right, Mom?"

Everyone was talking at once. And no one was listening to anyone else. It was exactly as it had always been. Looking at these wonderful people who had shared her life, Jillian realized that it was *she* who had changed.

"Maybe I'll surprise all of you and catch it myself."

All eyes turned to Jillian, but Lisa's grew the largest. Realization dawned slowly, her lips parting slightly, then easing into a smile. "Welcome back to the world of the living. And may the best woman win."

Travis, Cori and Allison walked to the side yard hand in hand in hand, Ivy, Lisa and Jillian following close behind. They stood amidst the throngs of single women, all of whom looked pretty intent upon taking the prize. Imagining the look on Luke's face if she should place that delicate bouquet in his big, work-roughened hands, something literally gave way inside Jillian.

The area surrounding her heart must have looked like one of those speed-recorded movies of a hundred delicate flowers opening their petals for the very first time. Certain she might just burst with anticipation, she squeezed Lisa's hand, ready for the traditional tossing of the bouquet. And the rest of her life to begin.

Gray. The color was everywhere, as far as the eye could see. The air in Jillian's rearview mirror was thick with gray dust, and ahead of her, gray clouds swirled together in the sky. The fence lining the country road was gray, too, and so were the occasional houses she passed.

Of all the colors of gray she'd seen so far, she could hardly wait to look into Luke's gray eyes. Fingering the object in her lap, she turned onto the lane leading to the

Carson homestead where Cletus had told her she would find Luke. The excitement bubbling inside her made her feel downright giddy. She rounded the curve in the driveway and caught her first glimpse of a black Stetson. Luke. Her first impulse was to call his name, but he glanced over his shoulder and looked at her, and she couldn't remember what she'd been about to say.

She climbed out of the car automatically, moving toward him as if being propelled by a force much larger than she was. The wind kicked up a little cyclone of loose dirt, swirling it straight at her. Blinking away the sting in her eyes, her steps slowed.

Luke wasn't sure, but a freight train might have been chugging through his chest. This was the moment he'd been waiting for all weekend, the moment that Jillian came back. Now that it had arrived, all he could do was stare and grin like an idiot.

Lord, she was a sight for sore eyes, with her hair swirling across one cheek and her skirt pressed close to her legs in undulating waves. He never realized how good redheads could look in pink. Of course, Jillian would have had his blood pounding through his body no matter what color she wore.

"You came back."

She started to nod, started to smile, and so did he. But then she glanced behind him.

"Luke, watch out!"

Something in her voice lowered his smile a notch. He heard a crash and the sound of splintering wood. The next thing he knew the bull he'd been examining from the outside of a wood-and-steel stanchion was bursting through boards and snorting his way toward Luke.

Jillian darted to the gate, her heart in her throat, a chant on her lips. The wind ripped Luke's hat from his head, tearing a scream from her lips at the same time.

"Luke. Run!"

She'd never seen a man move so fast or scale a steel gate with so little time to spare. He thudded to the ground in a heap, springing to his feet the instant he landed. She'd always known he could move like lightning. Today her heart supplied the thunder.

She'd never known anyone so brave as to place himself between her and a charging bull, but the feeling in the pit of her stomach was all too familiar. They took a few steps back when the bull rattled the gate. Jillian's heart lodged in her throat, but the gate held. As if to accent his sheer size and power, the bull snorted then stomped on Luke's hat.

"I was just getting that hat broke in."

Jillian knew Luke was trying to lighten the moment and did her best to give him a semblance of a smile. His hair looked freshly cut, the lines and angles in his face even more symmetrical than she remembered. One corner of his mouth raised as if he was infinitely glad to see her, the movement creasing one lean cheek.

"What do you say I go wash this dust off and take you out to dinner so we can celebrate your return in style?"

He turned to face her with the same easy grace and surefootedness that had just saved his life. Everything inside her went still, everything except the beating rhythm of her heart.

She should have known that a man who climbed into pens with large animals came face-to-face with danger now and then. But Luke had always seemed too strong, too light on his feet and ornery in his own right to get hurt. Now she knew just how close he came to danger. If he'd been three seconds slower, the bull would have won. Luke would have lost, and so would she.

All the anticipation that had bubbled inside her mere minutes ago turned to dread. She fought tears and a lump in her throat the size of a fist.

"What do you say, Jillian?"

Words wouldn't form, so she turned away without speaking.

"Jillian, where are you going?"

Luke had seen Jillian stop short and slowly turn to face him before, but if he lived to be a hundred, he'd never forget the way she did it this time, all "stiff upper lip" and stubborn pride. He felt his eyes narrow and every nerve ending in his body go on red alert.

"It was a mistake to come here. What I have to tell you can wait."

"Tell me now."

He didn't like the momentary wildness in her eyes, but when her chin came up another notch and the wildness was replaced by a look of stone, he liked it even less.

"The principal of the elementary school where I applied for a position came to Cori's wedding. She told me she's made her decision, and the job is mine for the taking."

The lift of her eyebrows seemed to say, "You asked, and I answered."

She walked to the car stiffly, climbed inside and started the engine. The only indication she gave that she was nervous was the way the tires churned up loose gravel as she pulled away.

Staring at the dust in the distance, Luke realized that there were two ways to be gored clear to the heart. And he'd come close to experiencing them both in one day.

He raked his fingers through his hair, already missing his hat. He'd missed Jillian a helluva lot more all weekend. And now, just like that, he was supposed to accept the fact that she was leaving for good? For lack of anything better to do, he let loose a string of expletives that had earned him a good mouth washing when he was ten. He wasn't ten anymore. He was thirty-five and in love, deeply, completely. Leave it to the only woman he'd ever loved to drive all the way back to Jasper Gulch just to tell him that she wasn't going to stay.

Something about that logic made him pause. It didn't make sense. He glanced from the bull to the place Jillian had parked. A splash of color caught his eye. Making a beeline for the driveway, he leaned down and scooped a bouquet of wilting yellow roses and dainty white ribbons off the ground.

She'd caught the bouquet.

Hope sprang to life within him. No matter what she said, she hadn't come here to tell him she was leaving. She came to tell him she loved him. Seeing that bull try to get into his back pocket must have changed her mind. Of all the rotten timing.

Agitated, Luke strode to the house, where he almost ran headlong into his father who was shouldering his way through the door, a suitcase tucked under each arm.

"Going someplace?" Luke asked.

Hugh Carson met his son's gaze. "If you can't bring Mohammed to the mountain, take the mountain to Mohammed."

"You're going to Oregon to see Mom?"

"With my hat in one hand and my heart in the other. It's about time, don't you think? I may be stubborn, but I'm not a complete fool. Take care of yourself, son. I'll call when I get there."

Luke stood on the back stoop of the house where he'd grown up, watching as his father's truck became a speck on the horizon.

If you can't bring Mohammed to the mountain, take the mountain to Mohammed.

The germ of an idea quickly grew into a full-fledged plan. He knew it wasn't going to be easy to convince Jillian that they belonged together, not after the close call she'd witnessed. But Luke had too much at stake to give up now.

He jumped into his truck and headed for his place on the edge of town. With adrenaline churning the acid in his stomach, he showered and shaved and planned. When he was ready, he climbed back into his truck, made a quick stop at the Jasper Gulch grocery store, then headed for Elm Street and the woman he loved.

Jillian Daniels. Prepare to meet your mountain.

Chapter Eleven

An hour later Luke was on his way to the library. Rumor had it that was where Jillian was. It was highly likely, since the library was about the only place in town he hadn't looked. She hadn't been at her house on Elm Street. And when he'd checked in the Jasper Gulch Clothing Store, Lisa said she hadn't seen her. Neither had Mel McCully at the diner or DoraLee down at the Crazy Horse. It was Cletus who finally pointed him toward the library. One of these days Luke would have to thank the old geezer. But not now. Now he had something much more important to do.

Boomer, who was hanging around in front of the barbershop, called, "Nice flowers."

One of the Anderson brothers yelled, "Hey, Luke, where's your hat?"

By the time Luke realized anyone had spoken, he saw a movement on the other side of the library window, and it was too late to reply. When the door opened and Jillian walked out, they both hesitated, wet their lips, swallowed.

The building now being used as the library had once been an assay office in the Black Hills. According to local legend and a journal kept by Jasper Carson, the founder of the town, he'd won the small, clapboard structure, along with the assay officer's widow, in a poker game and had brought both back here almost a hundred years ago. It was one of the Ladies Aid Society's least favorite versions of the tale.

The only excuse Luke had for thinking about it now was that a man's mind tended to wander when he found himself staring at the one woman in all the world he loved and had almost lost. Although he couldn't quite decipher the expression on Jillian's face, losing her wasn't going to be an option. He'd been rehearsing what he was going to say for over and hour, but suddenly he didn't know where to begin.

Isabell Pruitt chose that moment to come bustling through the library door. "Why, Luke Carson, I haven't seen you anywhere near our fine, though small, library in years. Aren't you glad the members of the Ladies Aid Society stood up for the citizens of Jasper Gulch and demanded that they appropriate enough tax dollars to keep the doors open at least three days a week? A town without a library is unthinkable. A mind is a terrible thing to waste. Don't you agree?"

Luke might have been able to come up with a passable rejoinder, but his gaze strayed back to the woman standing on the top step, and he knew only one thing. He had to talk to Jillian.

"Cletus McCully says we're just a bunch of biddies. Now you tell me what the church basement would be without the new curtains we made?"

He had to talk to Jillian. Alone. And he had to talk to her now.

"Why, at our next meeting I think I'll bring up the subject of... Luke, are you listening? Luke?"

"Later, Isabell."

"Well, I never!" The gray-haired spinster left in a huff, sputtering.

Jillian went down one step, and he went up one. Keeping his eyes on hers, he lifted one hand and said, "I think you dropped something out at the ranch."

Jillian tucked the book she'd checked out of the library under her arm, then accepted the wilted bridal bouquet from Luke's big hand. "Luke, there's something I have to tell you."

"Wait. There's something I have to say first."

"Really, there's something you should know..."

As was his way, he didn't let her finish. Instead, he brought his other hand from behind his back and tossed an apple a foot into the air. With a lift of his eyebrows, he said, "I've always wanted to be teacher's pet. What do you say, Jillian? Wanna play school?"

She did everything in her power to continue seething because he wouldn't give her an opportunity to say what was on her mind. Still, the area surrounding her heart felt especially warm.

Going up to the next step, he polished the apple on his chest pocket then slowly handed it to her. "I had to give you the bouquet because, no matter what you said this afternoon, I believe you brought it back from Madison for a reason."

"Luke..."

"And the apple," he rushed on, interrupting again, "because I think that principal made a fine choice."

The warmth in Luke's voice and his steadfast belief in her sent tears to Jillian's eyes. "What am I going to do with you?"

His head came up, along with one corner of his mouth. "The list is long and varied, believe me."

"I really…"

"Now I can't guarantee I'll be around forever, but I've gotta tell you the Carsons are a long-living lot. My great-great-grandfather, Jasper Carson, lived to the ripe old age of ninety-nine, his son, a hundred and one. My grandmother in Oregon is eighty-three. And to prove to you that I'm not completely inflexible, I want you to know that I have every intention of moving my practice out to Wisconsin."

"Luke, that won't be necessary."

His hands fell away from his hips and hung limply at his sides like a man who'd given it his best shot. And lost.

"Luke, let me explain."

Anger flashed across his features like lightning, forking in his eyes, clamping tight in his jaw. Bringing his head up, he said, "I've offered you everything that makes me whole. I want to marry you, to move with you to Madison." His lip curled as he continued. "I figured you were a helluva woman the first time I saw you, Jillian. I was even going to try to live with the fact that I'm not your first choice, that you'll always love Brian. But one thing I never figured you for was a coward."

Eyes still flashing, he closed his mouth, turned on his heel and stomped away.

For a full five seconds Jillian stood on the step with her mouth gaping open. But then her instincts took over. She closed her mouth and flounced after him. Grabbing his arm, she said, "Don't you walk away from me, Luke Carson. Now, if you'd shut up for half a minute and listen, you'd know that the reason it won't be necessary for you to move your practice to Wisconsin is because I'm not taking the job in Madison. I'm staying here. With you. And although I'll probably never be able to get a word in edgewise again, I'm going to ask you to marry me. You have to accept, too, because I saved your life when I alerted you to that charging bull this afternoon. According to local custom, that makes you mine for the asking.''

Luke could hardly believe his eyes or his ears. Jillian stood before him, her blue eyes flashing, her red hair waving in total disarray, her chest heaving. No woman had ever looked at him with so much glowing intensity in her eyes. No woman had ever spoken to him as if he'd darn well better listen. He'd known she was intelligent and strong, but until now he thought she'd been as patient as the day was long. Patient, hell. The redhead had a temper. In that instant he knew life was going to be a lot of things, but it was never going to be boring.

Desire, hot and lusty, came out of nowhere with a force that nearly blinded him. He took a step toward her, and darned if he didn't grin. ''And?'' he asked.

His simple question caught Jillian completely off guard. Good heavens. What had she said? What had she done?

She cast a quick glance all around and wished she hadn't. People up and down Main Street were standing on the sidewalks, whispering behind their hands or grinning from ear to ear.

She couldn't remember the last time she'd been so angry. Who was she trying to kid? She'd *never* been so angry. But then she'd never known another man who made her react this way. Luke Carson was an exasperating man, from the way he was standing there with his hands on his hips, his scuffed cowboy boots planted on the sidewalk, his hips jutted out in that arrogant, cocksure way he had. The nerve of him. To make her blow up in front of the entire town and then calmly stand there and ask, ''And?'' as if being told that he was hers for the asking was the most natural thing in the world.

What did he mean by that *and,* anyway? She went still for a moment, contemplating the possibilities.

The wind picked up, sifting through the short layers of his hair, fluttering his shirt collar around his neck. By the time she raised her eyes to his, her anger had evaporated into thin air.

The intensity in his eyes reached inside her, spreading to a place beyond her heart, to a place she couldn't name. She felt a curious sense of nostalgia, and yet she knew she'd never felt exactly this way, had never loved in exactly this way, had never felt so full and happy and complete.

Sashaying a tiny bit closer, she settled her bouquet, book and apple into one hand and reached to touch his cheek with the other. "Your life is mine for the asking. *And,*" she whispered with quiet emphasis, "I'm asking."

Luke hooked his hands behind her back and swung her off her feet. The bouquet got crushed, the apple bruised, the book's cover crinkled.

"Luke," she admonished, "Isabell is going to charge me a fine if I damage this cookbook."

"Cookbook?"

She was smiling when he set her on her feet. "I thought I'd start with *Cooking for Beginners.* I can't go around poisoning innocent children, not to mention my future husband, now can I?"

She expected him to laugh. Instead his expression was completely serious. "Husband. I like the sound of that."

"Does that mean you're accepting?"

Luke raised his head and let loose a yee-ha that brought a chorus of similar shouts from up and down Main Street. Sliding one hand into her hair, the other around her waist, he brought his mouth close to hers. "Yes, that means I'm accepting. Boy-oh-boy-oh-boy am I accepting."

He kissed her. Or she kissed him. It didn't matter which,

because their mouths were joined, and so were their hearts. The kiss didn't last long. Neither of them could contain their grins long enough for that.

Resting his forehead against hers, he said, "I don't care if you ever learn to cook, Jillian. I want you to have everything you want, everything you need. One of these days a teaching position is going to open up here in Jasper Gulch. In the meantime, I want you to marry me, live with me, laugh with me, and every now and then, argue with me. And when the time's right, I'd like to have a couple of kids. Would you do that, Jillian?"

Everyone on the street heard her laughter, but Luke was the only one who heard her whisper, "Try and stop me."

She tucked her hand behind his neck, drawing his face to hers for another kiss. This kiss was different from the others. It was filled with happiness, but the laughter gave way to something much more powerful and rich and vital.

He felt a touch on his shoulder, on his arm, on his back. They opened their eyes and, with their faces tilted toward the clouds, they watched tiny droplets of rain fall from the clouds, dotting their faces with water, warm and pure.

"Luke, it's raining."

They opened their mouths, and they knew how joy tasted. With laughter in their throats, they knew how it sounded. Looking at each other, they knew how it felt.

The droplets came down, soft, cleansing, bouncing off faded awnings, running down gutters, soaking everyone to the skin. Jillian looked all around her. Up and down Main Street, the citizens of Jasper Gulch danced jigs and laughed and carried on as if they'd never seen such a beautiful rain. Cletus was standing by his favorite bench, DoraLee in front of her saloon. Melody was smiling, and so was everyone else she could see.

"It's a perfect rain," Luke whispered, his voice close

to her ear. "No thunder or lightning. But it makes me miss my hat."

She laughed and shook her head and laughed some more. "Tomorrow, we'll get you another hat."

"And tomorrow," he said close to her ear, "we'll start to make wedding plans. Tomorrow, but not today."

"Today—"

"Today," he said, cutting in, "I want you to myself."

She took his big hand in hers and started toward his truck. "Where are we going?" he asked.

"Cletus hung an old-fashioned porch swing this morning. He called it a sparking bench. I had everything all planned. A simple meal, soft music, a swaying porch swing. I was going to tell you that I'd decided to stay in Jasper Gulch, and..."

"And I spoiled your plans."

"...and then," she continued as if he hadn't interrupted, "I was going to tell you that I've never been in love like this before, so that nothing else matters, except you and me and..."

"Really?"

She stopped walking and kissed him soundly on the mouth. Smiling, she resumed her pace, thinking that she had her own way to get a word in edgewise.

By the time they'd walked to the end of the block where his truck was parked and had driven to the house on Elm Street, they were both soaked to the skin. But neither of them felt cold. Together they sank onto the porch swing. Jillian sighed. And so did the world around her. The porch swing swayed, the rain surrounding them in a private, gray haze.

Luke fitted her head to his shoulder, loving the way her wet hair had darkened to deep red, loving the way her dress spread around her like a pale pink mist. He loved the way she smelled, the way she made him think. He even loved the way she made him mad. More than anything, he loved the way she colored his world.

"Luke, there's going to be one less bachelor in Bachelor Gulch."

"I always knew it would be me."

Jillian shook her head. She knew what she was in for with this rugged, exasperating, caring man. She was in for the best of the rest of her life. And the rest of her life had just begun.

*   *   *   *   *

Don't you fret. More wedding bells are about to ring in the next BACHELOR GULCH book. Be on the lookout for WYATT'S MOST WANTED WIFE available in August, only from Silhouette Romance.

twins
on the doorstep
by Stella Bagwell

When the Murdock sisters found abandoned twins
on their ranch-house doorstep, they had no clue the
little ones would lead them to love!

Come see how each sister meets her match—and how
the twins' family is discovered—in

THE SHERIFF'S SON (SR #1218, April 1997)

THE RANCHER'S BRIDE (SR #1224, May 1997)

THE TYCOON'S TOTS (SR #1228, June 1997)

TWINS ON THE DOORSTEP—a brand-new miniseries
by Stella Bagwell starting in April...
Only from

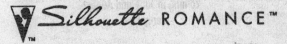

TWINS1

Bundles of Joy

Babies have a way of bringing out the love in everyone's hearts! And this summer, Silhouette Romance is presenting you with two wonderful love stories.

June:

THE TYCOON'S TOTS by Stella Bagwell (#1228)
Twins on the Doorstep continues! Chloe Murdock was set to adopt those sweet baby twins left on her doorstep—when their uncle, Wyatt Sanders, suddenly appeared. The handsome tycoon wanted to raise the tots as his own, but Chloe was soon hoping they'd all become part of a full-fledged family....

August:

BABY BUSINESS by Laura Anthony (#1240)
Millionaire Clay Barton suddenly had a baby to care for—and needed some help, fast! So when the lovely, capable Dr. Tobie Avery showed up, Clay thought he was in the clear. That is, until Tobie's womanly charms had this rugged daddy figure imagining the tempting pediatrician in a more permanent position—as his wife!

Don't miss these adorable Bundles of Joy,
coming in June and August,
only from

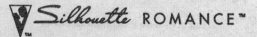

And the Winner Is...
You!

...when you pick up these great titles
from our new promotion at your
favorite retail outlet this June!

Diana Palmer
The Case of the Mesmerizing Boss

Betty Neels
The Convenient Wife

Annette Broadrick
Irresistible

Emma Darcy
A Wedding to Remember

Rachel Lee
Lost Warriors

Marie Ferrarella
Father Goose

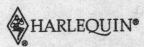 

AVAILABLE THIS MONTH FROM SILHOUETTE ROMANCE®

This summer, the legend
continues in Jacobsville

A LONG, TALL
TEXAN SUMMER

Three **BRAND-NEW** short stories

This summer, Silhouette brings readers a special
collection for Diana Palmer's LONG, TALL TEXANS
fans. Diana has rounded up three **BRAND-NEW**
stories of love Texas-style, all set in Jacobsville,
Texas. Featuring the men you've grown to love from
this wonderful town, this collection is a must-have
for all fans!

*They grow 'em tall in the saddle in Texas—and
they've got love and marriage on their minds!*

Don't miss this collection of original Long, Tall Texans
stories…available in June at your favorite retail outlet.

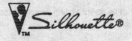

IT'S A MONTH OF WEDDED BLISS!

In July, Silhouette Romance is proud to present six irresistible novels about love and marriage. Don't miss:

#1234 *And Baby Makes Six* by Pamela Dalton
It's A Girl!

#1235 *Three Kids And A Cowboy* by Natalie Patrick
Second Chance At Marriage

#1236 *Just Say I Do* by Lauryn Chandler
Substitute Groom

#1237 *The Bewildered Wife* by Vivian Leiber
The Bride Has Amnesia!

#1238 *Have Honeymoon, Need Husband* by Robin Wells
Runaway Bride

#1239 *A Groom for Maggie* by Elizabeth Harbison
Green Card Marriage

Don't miss a single one, available in July, only from

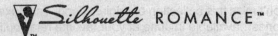

Silhouette ROMANCE™

Look us up on-line at: http://www.romance.net   WHIRL

New York Times Bestselling Authors

JENNIFER BLAKE
JANET DAILEY
ELIZABETH GAGE

Three *New York Times* bestselling authors bring you three very sensuous, contemporary love stories—all centered around one magical night!

It is a warm, spring night and masquerading as legendary lovers, the elite of New Orleans society have come to celebrate the twenty-fifth anniversary of the Duchaise masquerade ball. But amidst the beauty, music and revelry, some of the world's most legendary lovers are in trouble....

Come midnight at this year's Duchaise ball, passion and scandal will be...

Unmasked

Revealed at your favorite retail outlet in July 1997.

Silhouette
ROMANCE™

COMING NEXT MONTH

It's a month of your favorite wedding themes! Don't miss:

#1234 AND BABY MAKES SIX—Pamela Dalton
Fabulous Fathers/It's A Girl!
Single father Devlin Hamilton agreed to a *platonic* marriage with lovely Abby O'Reilly. Their children needed a real family—and Devlin and Abby could help each other without the added risk of true love. Until a surprisingly passionate wedding night led to a new family addition!

#1235 THREE KIDS AND A COWBOY—Natalie Patrick
Second Chance At Marriage
Playing the part of the loving wife wasn't difficult for Miranda Sykes. She still loved her soon-to-be ex-husband, and Brodie needed her to adopt the orphans he'd taken in. But Miranda hadn't realized that three kids and a cowboy just might change her mind about staying around forever!

#1236 JUST SAY I DO—Lauryn Chandler
Substitute Groom
A fake engagement to dashing Adam Garrett would finally rid once-jilted bride Annabelle of everyone's pity. But when sparks started to fly between her and her substitute groom, their arrangement didn't feel like a game anymore! Could Annabelle get Adam to just say "I do" for real?

#1237 THE BEWILDERED WIFE—Vivian Leiber
The Bride Has Amnesia!
Dean Radcliffe's nanny had lost her memory…and thought she was Dean's wife and mother of his children! Until Susan remembered the truth, the handsome single father had to play along, but could it be this bewildered woman was meant to *truly* be his wife?

#1238 HAVE HONEYMOON, NEED HUSBAND—Robin Wells
Runaway Bride
After jilting her two-timing fiancé, Josie Randall decided to go on her dude ranch honeymoon—alone. Falling for wrangler Luke O'Dell was the last thing she'd expected—but the brooding, stubborn rancher soon lassoed her love, and had her hoping this honeymoon could land Luke as a husband!

#1239 A GROOM FOR MAGGIE—Elizabeth Harbison
Green Card Marriage
A marriage of convenience to her arrogant boss was drastic, but Maggie Weller would do anything to stay with Alex Harrison—and care for his adorable little girl. But Maggie's green-card wedding led not only to a permanent position in Alex's home, but to a most *un*expected place in his heart!